One hot June afternoon o ... a call from LOVESWEPT ... my first book. I thought I ... happy but calm. I even took my family out to a restaurant to celebrate. Unfortunately, they had to bring me home immediately because I was hyperventilating. Not an entirely unexpected response when you realize your life is going to change.

The story concerned a beautiful actress, a baby, and a movie director who bore a resemblance to both George Lucas and Steven Spielberg. I made a number of mistakes in that first book. The plot was pure fantasy at a time when everyone in publishing was looking for "realistic" romance. I also fell in love with a secondary character, Jake Dominic, and knew I had to give him his own story. Another mistake; everyone knew you should never make secondary characters that strong in a small book.

The book was titled *The Love Formula*, which LOVESWEPT promptly changed to *Stormy Vows*. They did it gently and diplomatically as was proper with a fledgling author who was passionately possessive of every word and character in her books.

Ten years and many, many books have passed. I still make mistakes and they're still very gentle with me.

Happy Anniversary, LOVESWEPT.

Iris Johansen

WHAT ARE *LOVESWEPT* ROMANCES?

They are stories of true romance and touching emotion. We believe those two very important ingredients are constants in our highly sensual and very believable stories in the LOVESWEPT line. Our goal is to give you, the reader, stories of consistently high quality that may sometimes make you laugh, sometimes make you cry, but are always fresh and creative and contain many delightful surprises within their pages.

Most romance fans read an enormous number of books. Those they truly love, they keep. Others may be traded with friends and soon forgotten. We hope that each LOVESWEPT romance will be a treasure—a "keeper." We will always try to publish

LOVE STORIES YOU'LL NEVER FORGET
BY AUTHORS YOU'LL ALWAYS REMEMBER

The Editors

Loveswept ® 622

STAR-SPANGLED BRIDE

IRIS JOHANSEN

BANTAM BOOKS
NEW YORK · TORONTO · LONDON · SYDNEY · AUCKLAND

STAR-SPANGLED BRIDE

A Bantam Book / June 1993

ISBN 0-553-44184-1

Published simultaneously in the United States and Canada

Bantam Books are published by Bantam Books, a division of
Bantam Doubleday Dell Publishing Group, Inc. Its trademark,
consisting of the words "Bantam Books" and the portrayal of
a rooster, is Registered in U.S. Patent and Trademark Office
and in other countries. Marca Registrada. Bantam Books,
1540 Broadway, New York, New York 10036.

PRINTED IN THE UNITED STATES OF AMERICA

OPM   0 9 8 7 6 5 4 3 2 1

PROLOGUE

Mekhit, Turkey
May 9, 1983

The darkness was absolute, pressing down on her, taking away her breath.

Her hands clawed weakly at the block of concrete barring the entrance, but it was too heavy to shift. Why did she keep trying? She was going to die. Her throat was raw with screaming, but no one had heard her.

"Are you there? Dammit, answer me. Talk to me." A man's voice shouting, strong and angry.

"Here." It came out a hoarse croak. "Help me. . . ."

"I'm trying to help. I've been trying since I heard you two hours ago." She could hear the shifting of concrete slabs. "Are you hurt?"

"I don't think so." It was difficult to tell. At first, she had been aware of pain, but time and terror had blurred sensation. "Arm hurts . . . a little. Why did the . . . parking garage blow up?"

"The entire world blew up," he said. "It was a seven-point-five earthquake on the Richter scale. The hotel collapsed. We've been trying to dig survivors out for the last eight hours."

Was that how long it had been? It had seemed forever, an eternity of forevers. An earthquake. Why hadn't that possibility occurred to her? Her first thought had been a missile.

"Is there anyone else there with you?"

"No." It was always her job to make sure the rendezvous was deserted. Evan said no one ever suspected kids. "I'm alone."

"You're fading away. Keep talking. What's your name?"

What was the name on her passport this time? she wondered hazily. Anita . . . Anita something. "Anita."

That seemed enough for him. "I'm Gabe. Can you tell me how close you were to the door when the quake hit?"

She tried to remember. "Close. I started running. . . . I didn't reach it in time."

"How close?"

"Three feet . . ."

"Then we're almost there. Hold on."

How could she hold on when there was nothing to hold on to? Just darkness and the destruction around her. "Could you hurry? I'm . . . afraid."

"There's nothing to be afraid of."

A sudden flare of anger pierced her panic. "Not for you. You don't have a hotel sitting on top of you."

There was a moment of surprised silence and then Gabe chuckled. "Touché. It was a stupid remark. I must be getting tired. Of course, you're afraid. Try to get your mind off it. You're American?"

The passport said Spanish. "No."

"You sound American."

"Spanish. English mother."

"I'm American. Texas. I was born and raised in Plano. Do you know where that is?"

"No."

"It's a little town right outside of Dallas, almost like a suburb. Well, it used to be a small town. Now it's growing like a mushroom after a rainstorm. You're not talking."

"I'm listening. I can't do both."

A sudden rush of air touched her face as one of the blocks was shifted to the side and she saw the conelike beam of a flashlight through the narrow opening. Hope flared and she tried to wriggle forward. "You're here. I can see the light."

"I told you."

Then the sound of movement ceased and she heard low voices.

Something was wrong, she thought desperately. Nothing was happening.

"Anita," Gabe called. "We've reached some heavy metal beams barring the entrance. We have to go and get more help."

"You're going to leave me?" She couldn't keep the panic out of her voice.

"Only for a little while. I'll be right back."

"I'm sorry," she said quickly. "It's all right. I'll be fine."

Another discussion and then Gabe said quietly, "It's okay. I'll stay." He thrust his hand through the opening. "Here, take my hand."

She reached out and his hand closed over hers in the darkness.

Strength. Safety.

Her heart stopped its frantic pounding.

"All right?" Gabe asked quietly.

"Yes." The hand grasping her own was big, powerful. She tried to identify the shape and textures of the anchor that was keeping her from the terror; light calluses on the ball of the hand and the forefinger, long fingers, strong tendons. Most of all she was conscious of the warmth and strength. "I'm sorry I lost it for a minute. I'm not usually this cowardly."

"You don't usually have a hotel sitting on you." Humor colored his voice as he repeated her words. "I thought we agreed you had a right to be afraid. I've been in better situations myself."

Her grip on his hand tightened. "It's just that it feels . . . like a coffin."

"You simply have to remember that it's not. In the daylight it would look like a rubble heap at the local dump."

Her laugh was half-hysterical. "And I'm part of the trash."

"No, you're not trash. You're a human being and your life is very, very precious."

He meant it. She did have value for him even though she was a stranger. The realization caused her rising panic to abate.

"What are you doing in Mekhit?" he asked.

He was trying to keep her talking, trying to

keep the fear at bay, she realized. "I was on vacation from school."

"School? Which university do you attend?"

"None. I'm not old enough."

"How old are you?"

"Fourteen."

"Then what in hell were you doing alone in a parking garage at three o'clock in the morning?"

She couldn't think of a plausible answer, so she asked a question of her own to divert him. "Why are you here?"

"I'm a reporter and I was staying at the hotel. I was having a drink in the bar in the lobby when the hotel started shaking like a belly dancer. I was luckier than you; I made it to the street before it toppled like a house of cards. The entire town is a disaster."

Evan had been waiting in the car outside the hotel. If Gabe had survived, Evan was probably all right too. She hadn't really been worried. Evan always said he had nine lives and she herself had seen him use up at least three of them.

"I hear them coming. We'll have you out in no time." He started to release her hand.

"No!" She grabbed frantically at the lifeline he was taking away. "Don't go."

"It's not safe for me to—" He stopped and then said, "I'm not going to leave you." His big hand tightened around hers once more. "See, I'm right here and I'm going to stay here. Hold on to me."

That feeling of infinite safety washed over her again. Warmth in the cold. Safety in danger. Light in the darkness.

She would hold on to him.

She would hold on forever.

ONE

"It's too dangerous." Evan's gaze slid away from Ronnie's face. "I've changed my mind."

"The hell you have." Ronnie Dalton smothered the spark of panic her father's words ignited within her and kept her expression blank. She knew Evan would pounce on any show of weakness on her part as an excuse to abandon the plan. He would respond only to absolute determination. "No way, Evan."

"Falkner's too hot to handle. You'll get us both killed."

"You're not even going to be there. You make the final payoff and then head for the border."

"That doesn't mean they won't come after me if they suspect I was in on it. These terrorists are not ones to fool around with." He frowned. "I don't even know why I let you talk me into this."

"For Lord's sake, we're Falkner's last hope," she said, exasperated. "The discussions have broken down and they'll kill him if we don't get him out of there."

Evan shook his head. "Falkner's too important for them to waste. The Red December would have everyone from the CIA to the Associated Press breathing down their necks."

"They've had them breathing down their necks for over a year and it hasn't bothered them. The Red December are fanatics. Who should know that better than you?"

"The government will start negotiations again. You told me yourself that everyone in the media is in an uproar about his kidnapping. Politicians can't take that kind of heat without caving in to pressure."

"It will be too late. The terrorists have already lost face. Those idiots in Washington have blown it."

"What if they have? Why should I care?" he burst out. "It's not my responsibility. You may have a king-size case of hero worship for the man, but he's nothing to me."

"He *is* your responsibility."

"You're talking as if I personally kidnapped

the bastard," he said sulkily. "You're not my conscience, Ronnie. I'd have thought you would have
learned that by now. You can't change me and I
won't march to your drummer."

She *had* learned that a long time ago, she
thought wearily, but this time she couldn't let
him wander away without his cleaning up his
mess. "He's an extraordinary man. He deserves
to live, Evan." His expression didn't change and
she added in desperation, "I promise I won't ask
your help again."

He gazed at her a moment and then a sudden
boyish grin lit his heavy features. "The hell you
won't. Whenever you decide you can use me to
get a story, you'll be right there trailing behind
me just like you did when you were a kid."

She smiled. "Well, maybe . . ." She pushed on
quickly, heartened by the sign of softening. "But
you've got to do this. There's practically no risk
for you."

"Why are you being so damn stubborn? You
don't even know the man." He tilted his head and
gazed at her curiously. "Or do you?"

"What do you mean?" she asked warily. "I
already told you I didn't."

"Falkner has a pretty hot reputation with the
ladies," he said slyly. "I thought he might have

shown you sex is more fun than taking pictures."

"Maybe for you," she retorted, then went on quickly, "Gabe Falkner is a legend. I don't have to know him to know the news business would be a lot worse without him. What other boss would trade himself to a bunch of fanatical idiots like the Red December to free two of his reporters?"

He stared at her in astonishment. "Good God, I believe I was right about your case of hero worship. I thought I'd brought you up with more sense."

"No such thing," she countered. "That was just a comment. I'm only after the story. Any photojournalist in the world would risk their necks to film Falkner's escape."

"Film?" He snorted in disgust. "You never mentioned filming. I suppose I should have known. You'll be lucky to get away without being blown to bits, and you're thinking of taking pictures?"

"Only if it's convenient," she said.

"There's nothing convenient about this craziness. Falkner's ankles will be chained so that he'll barely be able to shuffle. He's been beaten and starved, so that he'll scarcely be able to function much less react quickly enough to give you any help."

"You underestimate him. He's hard as nails."

Evan thought for a moment before acceding. "Maybe you're right. Mohammed says he's one tough bastard."

He was more than tough, Ronnie thought. He was larger than life in every sense of the word. After spending five years as a foreign correspondent, Gabe Falkner had taken a small Texas radio station he had inherited from his father and built it into a worldwide news network, comprised of newspapers, magazines, and a cable news network that was currently giving CNN a run for its money.

Though he strode ruthlessly over anyone who stood in his way, Falkner was known to be absolutely fair in his business practices and to battle tooth and nail to protect his employees. In a world where newsmen were evaluated and discarded by computer polls, Falkner exhibited an old-fashioned paternalism. He chose excellent people, paid them excellent money, and then gave them unlimited protection. In return he inspired a loyalty unprecedented among the media.

"Even if Falkner can help," Evan said, "even if everything goes right, it will be a miracle if you can get him away and into hiding. If you get in a jam, you can't rely on the Said Ababa government. They'll just look the other way. They give lip service to Washington, but they're too afraid of the Red December to interfere."

"I know that," Ronnie muttered impatiently. "Why are you rehashing old news? Nothing is going to go wrong; we've got everything covered."

"We could wait another day," Evan coaxed. "Maybe Washington will come through."

"And maybe those murderers will decide to shoot Falkner in the head tonight." She shook her head. "And if they didn't, you might not be able to find where they'll take him tomorrow night. They never keep him in any one place more than twenty-four hours." She stood up, jammed her hands into the pockets of her leather flight jacket, and said belligerently, "Now stop arguing with me. You agreed to do it and we're going to do it tonight. I'll be in that alcove on the Street of the Camels at eleven tonight. If you don't send the help you promised, they'll catch me and have two newspeople to execute." A sudden mischievous smile lit her face. "And then you'd have to go to my funeral and you know how you hate that kind of hoopla."

"What makes you think I'd go?"

"Because you know I'd haunt you if you didn't."

"You'd do it too." He scowled and with reluctance said, "All right. We'll go on with it, but don't expect anything else of me. I'll make the payment to Mohammed and Fatima and then I'm on my way."

Her relief was immeasurable. "That's all I ask." Then after a moment's hesitation, she added, "You're sure Mohammed is a good enough shot?"

Evan nodded. "It will be close range." He smiled crookedly. "I'm surprised you sanctioned shooting the guards. Isn't your heart bleeding for them?"

"I don't like it, but there's no other way." A shadow crossed her face. "And their hearts didn't bleed when they blew up that busload of schoolchildren last month." So much violence, so many tears in the world. No matter how often she was forced to face it, she never got used to it.

She impulsively bent down and brushed a light kiss on her father's forehead. "Thanks, Evan."

He stiffened at the gesture. "You must be more worried about this than I thought, if you're getting mushy on me."

"I'm never mushy. I just thought . . ." She

turned on her heel and headed for the front door. "Oh, what the hell."

"Be careful."

She glanced over her shoulder in surprise. "That sounds a bit mushy too."

He shook his head. "Purely selfish. I just hate funerals."

Funerals, sentiment, and every other convention, including the responsibilities of fatherhood, she thought with a tiny pang. She quickly dismissed both the thought and the accompanying hurt. What was wrong with her today? She had no more need of a father now at twenty-four than she had when she was ten. She had been brought up to be completely independent of Evan and everyone else. That was how Evan liked it and that was the way she liked it too.

She saluted him jauntily. "I'll try not to inconvenience you. See you next time."

She didn't wait for an answer but quickly left the hotel room, cursing herself for the affectionate gesture that had embarrassed both Evan and herself. She couldn't remember the last time she had kissed her father. El Salvador? Probably not. Beneath that easygoing facade he was completely self-centered and found physical demonstrations unappealing.

Well, so did she. She didn't need any affection from anyone. She was just as self-centered and tough as Evan and she had reached out to him only because she was a little frightened about tonight.

Who was she kidding? She was terrified. Every argument Evan had used had hit dead center. If she was smart, she would abandon the plan, turn her back on Falkner, and get the hell out of Said Ababa.

The latest picture the Red December had released of Gabe Falkner rushed back to her. His broad face was thinner than before his capture, the flesh bruised, one eye blackened, his dark hair tousled. Yet despite the obvious mistreatment he conveyed the impression of boundless strength. He was staring into the camera with intimidating coldness and a recklessness that had caught her imagination. She had replayed the news tape dozens of times, and each time she saw it, maternal ferocity had surged through her. Blast it, a man like that didn't deserve to be used as a punching bag by those creeps. Even if Evan hadn't been involved, even if the opportunity for an Emmy hadn't beckoned, she would probably still be here.

Not because of any mushy feelings of nobility, as Evan had charged, but out of respect for an extraordinary man, her own professional ambition, and a certain amount of gratitude. If those reasons had been powerful enough to bring her to this point, then they should be enough to make her go through with the escape plan.

If she could just get over this damned panic soaring through her.

The Jeep containing Falkner and his two guards stopped at the top of the Street of the Camels.

Ronnie drew a breath of relief. Ten minutes late. She had been afraid they had changed their plans.

She edged forward in the alcove and focused her camcorder on Falkner as he stepped out of the Jeep. The light from the street lamp played over him. Lord, he was big. Almost six foot five and built like Schwarzenegger. The jeans and cotton sweater he wore were soiled and ragged, but they revealed the enormous strength and power of his thighs and shoulders. His hawklike features reflected the same toughness. She couldn't see his eyes from where she was, but knew they were a pale icy blue.

The guards were evidently well aware of that power because his hands were manacled and his ankles chained so that he could walk with only a shuffling gait. One of the guards said something to Falkner and then pushed him to start him down the street. Falkner turned and looked at him. It was just a stare, but the guard faltered and then started to curse as he prodded Falkner with his automatic rifle.

Great stuff, Ronnie thought absently as she continued filming. She could almost hear the voice-over—Falkner, dominant even in captivity.

The three men were heading toward her, their destination the house at the end of the block. She was located at the halfway point. Reluctantly she turned off the camcorder and put it in her camera bag.

The men were now a hundred yards from where she stood.

Bracing herself, Ronnie reached behind her, silently opened the door she had previously oiled, and took the smoke grenade from her jacket pocket.

Fifty yards.

She cast an anxious glance at the second-story window across the street. Mohammed had better be as good a shot as Evan had said. He would have to pick off both guards within a matter of seconds to keep them from turning on Falkner.

Five yards.

She pulled the pin from the smoke grenade with her teeth.

The first shot!

The guard on the far side of Falkner fell to the ground.

She hurled the smoke bomb down the street.

The sickening *thunk* of a bullet hitting flesh as Mohammed's second bullet struck the remaining guard.

Billows of smoke suddenly obscured everything in the narrow street.

She darted out of the alcove. Her hand grasped Falkner's arm. "Hurry!"

He didn't question her. "Right." He let her pull him into the alcove and through the open doorway.

She slammed the door, shot the bolt, and then moved down the corridor. "Follow me. We have two minutes before the men from the house will get here and another two minutes before the smoke clears enough for them to start a search. There's a trapdoor in the basement that leads to a fruit cellar. I've cut an exit out of the cellar that leads to a storm drain." She fired the words as she hurried down a curving staircase, then into the basement. "Can you manage a ladder in those chains?"

"I could manage to climb Mount Everest if it meant getting away from these bastards," he said grimly, his gaze searching her blackened face. "Who are you? CIA?"

They had reached the fruit cellar, and she led him to the cut-out exit. She shook her head as she started down the ladder. "Later."

"What's your name?" he persisted.

"Ronnie. Ronnie Dalton." She waited for him at the bottom of the ladder and then played the flashlight on the drainage pipe. "You first."

He looked at the opening skeptically. "It looks pretty small."

"You'll fit. I measured it."

"Very efficient." He got down on his hands and knees and began to crawl through the pipe.

She waited until he was several yards ahead and then went in, shutting the camouflaged door behind her. "Hurry!" she whispered. "We have to be at the end of the pipe in four minutes."

"And where does it exit?"

"Two blocks north."

"You have a car waiting?"

"No."

"Why the hell not?"

"Stop questioning me and move!"

"I'll move, but I'll be damned if I'll stop questioning you. This is my life and I'm not risking it for any half-baked plan that—"

"It's the only hope you've got," she said in exasperation. "I've got it covered. Trust me."

"Under these kind of circumstances I don't trust anyone but myself."

"Well, maybe it's time you changed. You didn't do so well getting away from them on your own. It's not— Why are you stopping?"

"I've reached the end of the pipe." He moved cautiously out onto the street. "No one in sight."

"There will be soon. This entire area will be crawling with those scum once they radio for reinforcements."

He stood up and reached out a hand to pull her to her feet. "Then let's get out of here."

She moved quickly ahead of him down the street, turned left and then right. She heard the jangle of his chains as he shuffled behind her. After the third block he muttered testily, "Are we supposed to walk all the way to the border?"

"If I say so." She turned left again, moved swiftly down the alley, threw open a door, and gestured for him to enter. "In here."

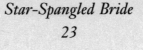

Fatima waited in the hall just inside the door. "You're late," she said sourly. "If you'd arrived two minutes later, you would have found the door locked. I told Evan I would take no unnecessary chances." She locked the door, then turned on her heel and walked quickly down the dimly lit corridor. "Come with me."

"What is this place?" Falkner asked.

"It's a bordello," Ronnie said. "We thought it would be safer for you to hide in plain sight. Here's the scenario. You're a customer and I'm one of Fatima's women."

Fatima threw open a door. "You'd better do it right," she told Ronnie grimly. "Or we'll all end up corpses."

"And that charming lady is the madam?" Falkner asked as the door closed behind Fatima.

Ronnie nodded. "Fatima al-Radir." She gestured toward the bed. "Sit down, I have to get those chains off."

"Gladly." He sat down, studying his rescuer. Not that there was much to study. Except for glittering wide-set hazel eyes and a slightly turned-up nose, he could discern little of her blackened face. Her thin body was dressed in black trousers and shirt and a sock cap that completely covered her hair. "And how do you intend to get rid of these chains? Do you have a file tucked in your bag?"

"Better." She knelt at his feet, fumbled in her camera bag, and pulled out a tiny key. "You'll be out of these in a minute."

"How well prepared you are." His gaze narrowed on her blackened face. "How do you happen to have—"

"There!" she interrupted as the lock opened on his ankle manacles. "Now give me your wrists."

He extended his hands. "And how did you know where I'd be tonight?"

"I never reveal my sources," she said lightly. "Deepthroat would never forgive me."

"You're a reporter?"

She nodded as she took the manacles off his hands. "Photojournalist."

"One of my people?"

"My people," she repeated. "I heard you were possessive about your employees."

"Well, are you?"

She shook her head. "Free-lance."

"You're taking a hell of a risk to get a story."

"I'm after an Emmy," she said flippantly. "Go get in the shower. I'll have Fatima get rid of these manacles. Throw out your clothes and I'll get rid of those too." She reached into the bag and handed him a small case. "False beard and eyebrows, brown contact lenses. Those blue eyes are a dead giveaway." She grimaced. "Oops, wrong word."

"I find it very apt under the circumstances," he told her as he took the case. "Am I on a schedule for this too?"

She picked up the manacles and headed to the door. "Seven minutes. Your old friends should be here within ten to search the house."

"Let's hope they keep to your agenda and not their own." He moved toward the bathroom. "I trust you're going to wash off that black stuff and get into something more appropriate?"

"Of course. Don't be stupid."

"I'm not known to be stupid." He slammed the door and began peeling off his clothes. Dammit, he knew he should be grateful since the woman had saved his neck, but there was something about Ronnie Dalton that rubbed his nerves like high-grade sandpaper. Her air of crisp decisiveness and aggressiveness made him want to reach out and shake her.

He stepped beneath the shower and let the lukewarm water run over him. He wasn't usually so unfair. Women had the right to be just as aggressive as men in this world. Face it, he probably would have been antagonistic toward anyone whose hands held his life. He liked to be in control and he'd had a bellyful of pent-up frustration and helplessness during this last year. But that wasn't Ronnie Dalton's fault, and he would have to submerge his natural instincts and work with her if they were going to get out of this alive.

"Geez, can't you hurry up?" she called through the door.

He gritted his teeth. "You gave me seven minutes. It's only been five." Gratitude, he reminded himself as he turned off the shower. After donning his disguise and wrapping a towel around his waist, he stepped out of the bathroom.

He saw she was in bed, leaning back against a high oak headboard that was as scarred and chipped as the other meager furniture in the room.

He stopped in shock.

She looked not a day over sixteen. Her skin glowed with fresh scrubbing and seemed as rose-petal soft as a baby's. Her golden hair was short and curled riotously about her face. The sheet was pulled up to her shoulders, but she was obviously nude beneath the thin cover.

"You look—"

"I know, I know," she said impatiently. "Like something from one of the old-time Gibson girl ads. I can't help it. Get into bed."

"I'm not sure I should," he said even as he slipped under the sheet and threw the towel aside. "How the hell old are you?"

"Twenty-four." She reached over to the bedside table and plucked a dark shining object from its surface, which proved to be a long black wig. After putting it on, she commenced to tuck her short blond curls underneath it. "This should make me look older."

"Wrong," he corrected. "Instead of looking like a Christmas-card angel, you've only turned into a nursery-school dropout."

"Really?" She frowned. "Well, it will have to do. Maybe they'll think you're one of those men who like young girls." She lifted the pillow to reveal a revolver. "A Magnum .357. We don't want to use it unless we have to, but it will blow a good-sized hole."

"Quite a good-sized hole. You're familiar with guns?"

"I grew up with them. When most kids were going to school, I was learning how to assemble an Uzi."

"Interesting."

"If I have to blow anyone away, head for the bathroom. That window opens onto the alley."

"You appear to have everything researched."

"I told you I wasn't stupid. I want to live as much as you do."

Her hand was opening and closing nervously on the sheet. "Now, when we hear them, you move over me and pretend we're doing it. Don't turn fully around, but it would be smart to let them get a glimpse of your beard."

"Misdirection." He stretched out and willed himself to relax. "I'll handle it."

"Do you speak Said Ababan? You should—"

"I said I'll handle it." He tried to keep the edge from his tone. "I assure you I learned to be very fluent in Said Ababan obscenities over the last year."

"You'll have to disguise your voice. They must be able to recognize it after all these months."

"For Lord's sake, I'm fully aware of—" He stopped as he noticed the rapid pounding of the pulse in her throat. She was frightened, he realized suddenly. Scared as hell and talking feverishly to keep from admitting it to him and to herself. The knowledge completely disarmed him. Why, she was only a kid and about as tough as his six-year-old niece, Daisy. He felt a rush of protectiveness ripple through him. "I'll watch it," he said quietly. "Now relax. There's nothing to do but wait."

She drew a deep breath. "I hate waiting."

"So do I, but I've learned to cope with it." Her skin had a silky sheen like that usually seen only in very young children, and he suddenly felt an urge to reach out and touch her. He found an excuse. His index finger tapped a small scar on her right shoulder. "What's this?"

"Bullet wound." She moistened her lips. "El Salvador."

He felt an odd surge of anger. "Who the hell sent you into that hellhole?"

"I sent myself," she said absently, her gaze fixed on the door. "And I got the footage."

"Wonderful," he said, his voice caustic. "And you also got a bullet."

The rough edge to his words must have startled her, for she turned to look at him in bewilderment. "Why are you so angry? There were plenty of your reporters in El Salvador."

"But they weren't—" He stopped. He didn't know why he was so angry. She was right; he had sent many of his people into danger. Risk was accepted as part of a reporter's life. Yet there was something so fragile and vulnerable about Ronnie Dalton despite her air of tough bravado that the thought of her in danger made him—

"It's my face, isn't it?" She grimaced. "I've had to fight this cherub's mug all my life. No one wants to take me seriously."

"You're still pretty young. It's not been a very long battle." He touched the scar again, his finger rubbing gently. "This isn't a fresh wound. How old were you when you got the scar?"

"Eighteen." She looked down at his finger. "I wish you wouldn't do that; it makes me feel . . . funny."

Touching her didn't make him feel funny, it made him horny as hell. He could feel himself hardening and was abruptly conscious of a lemony scent clinging to her, of her slight breasts thrusting beneath the thin sheet.

Crazy. He was probably only minutes away from another encounter with those Middle Eastern thugs and he wanted only to mount the woman and drive into her like a rutting stallion. Hell, maybe not so crazy. It was instinct for every species, when faced with death, to want to procreate. At least there was no doubt *he* wanted to.

"You're not—" She stopped when she heard the sound of raised voices in the hall. "They're here!"

He moved swiftly over her.

TWO

Warm hard flesh against her own.

Shock. Fear.

Ronnie was conscious her heart was pounding so hard it made her breath come in short, painful pants.

"You're shaking," he whispered. "Take it easy, everything will be all right."

"I know that." She swallowed and added, "Maybe."

His head lifted. "They're opening all the doors." He parted her thighs and moved between them. "Wrap your legs around me. Quick!"

She obeyed him without thinking, her thighs closing around his hips. Shocking hardness. Her eyes widened and her gaze flew to his face. "Why, you're—"

"Adrenaline has that effect on me. It doesn't mean anything," he muttered.

"It feels like it means something very—"

The door of their room flew open.

She couldn't see anything beyond his shoulder.

He turned his head so that only his bearded cheek would be revealed and shouted something in Said Ababan in a guttural tone.

There was an answering curse from the intruders and then the door slammed shut.

She went limp with relief. She whispered, "You'd better not move until we're sure they're gone."

"I'm not going anywhere," he said, his voice still thick and guttural. Then his hands fastened on her shoulders and he added, "We could make it even more believable." His palms began to move in a caressing, yearning movement. "Lord, you're soft. . . ."

And he was iron hard; the muscles of his chest and abdomen felt like steel pressed against her. Evan had said Falkner had exercised for hours every day in captivity and she could believe it as she felt the tough corded textures of him. She gazed up at him in fascination. The brown beard and contact lenses disguised him and yet they were not the cause of the sense of strangeness she felt. It came from Gabe Falkner himself, who was turning out to be a different, more vulnerable man than any she had imagined. His chest was moving rapidly, lifting and falling with each breath; his cheeks were flushed and hollowed with hunger.

His hips moved with the same yearning movement as his hands on her shoulders, and she felt a tingle of heat start between her thighs when he nestled even closer into that most intimate part of her. "Lord, I want *in!*" he said through his teeth. "Let me—"

She felt dazed, chained, unable to stir. She shook her head as much to clear it as to refuse him. "No, it's not—"

"No?" He froze in place. "Okay." He drew a deep ragged breath. "I hear you. My body isn't paying much attention, but I'm not going to rape you." His teeth sank into his lower lip. "Just lie perfectly still and I'll be all right."

Dimly she heard the uproar continuing on in the hall; the beating of his heart sounded louder, stronger, filling the room.

"Talk to me," he said.

She didn't know if she was capable of speech. "What do you want me to say?" she asked breathlessly.

"I couldn't care less. What is Ronnie short for? Veronica?"

"It's just Ronnie. My father wanted a boy."

"Why?"

"He thought a girl would be inconvenient. I was a big disappointment until he found out he could treat me like a boy anyway. Are they gone yet?"

"Not yet," he said in a hoarse voice. "I can still hear them at the other end of the hall. What about your mother?"

"She divorced my father when I was three."

"And left you?"

"For her a baby was an inconvenience, period. No matter what the sex."

"Sex..." he repeated. "I believe it's a mistake to mention that word under the present circumstances."

She laughed shakily. "Jed always did say I had a talent for blurting out the wrong thing at the wrong time."

He stiffened. "Who the hell is Jed?"

"They're gone," Fatima declared as she opened the door and marched into the room.

"Thank God!" Gabe pushed the sheet down and moved off Ronnie, stopping at her side.

Fatima raised her brows. "Your time with

her shouldn't have proved that unpleasant. She is skinny but not that bad." Her gaze went to his lower body and she grinned. "No, you do not find her too ugly."

Ronnie reached down to pull the sheet back over her naked body. "You've posted a lookout?"

Fatima nodded. "But I don't think they will be back. They've gone to search the house next door. I will send you food and wine."

"Will we be safe here?" Gabe asked.

Ronnie shrugged. "Safer than on the streets. They'll be stopping everyone for the next few hours. Evan has arranged for a Jeep to meet us at the edge of the bazaar at seven in the morning. It will be so busy there that we'll hardly be noticed."

"Evan?"

"My father." Ronnie wound the sheet around her and stood up. "I'll go get dressed."

"Stay here." Fatima turned. "Someone might see you and I don't need word of any strangers wandering around the place. I'll get the clothes Evan brought for both of you."

Ronnie stood uncertainly as the door closed behind Fatima before forcing herself to turn back to Gabe. He was lying there totally nude, she realized with shock. Big, brawny, unashamed, and completely male. Very male. She could feel the heat in her cheeks as she glanced away from him and said with bravado, "It's too bad the circumstances aren't different. Evan says Fatima's women are the best in the Middle East. You could take the edge off before—"

"Take the edge off?" Gabe repeated.

"That's what Evan calls it." Blast it, she wished Fatima would hurry with those clothes. She didn't look at him as she plopped down on the bed and retrieved her camera bag from under it. "I think it's one of his more apt phrases. It pretty much says it all, doesn't it? Sex gets rid of all the tension and lets a person get on with the important things."

"If you view sex so casually, why the hell didn't you let me—" He stopped and then, spacing each word carefully, said, "I believe we'd better talk about something else."

"Or not talk at all." She reached into her bag and with a flourish pulled out a deck of cards. "Poker?"

"You play?"

"Sure." She began to shuffle the cards. Damn, she hoped he wouldn't notice the slight tremor in her hands. "I'm terrific."

He sat up and crossed one muscular leg over the other. She wished he hadn't done that. It disturbed her. Now he looked like a naked sultan lolling in his harem, bringing all kinds of erotic thoughts to her mind.

He studied her for a moment and then smiled curiously. "Do you know, I believe I'm beginning to agree with you."

Gabe picked up his cards and, without looking at Ronnie, asked casually, "By the way, who is this Jed?"

"Jed Corbin."

He glanced up swiftly. "*The* Jed Corbin?"

She nodded. "We work together. Jed's fantastic."

"I agree. He's one of the best anchors in the business. I tried to lure him away to my network three years ago."

"Really? Jed never told me."

"Does he usually tell you everything?"

"Not as much as he should. He worries too much about his crew." She grinned at him. "Like you."

"You can never worry too much when you're asking your people to put their lives on the line."

He threw down a card, and Ronnie dealt him a new one. "Why haven't I heard about you? When I was investigating Corbin before offering him a job, I studied most of his stories. I don't remember seeing your name on the credits."

"I like to keep a low profile."

"Emmy Award seekers don't hide their lights under a bushel," he said flatly.

She could have bitten her tongue. Lord, he was sharp. She had forgotten she'd made that flippant remark, but evidently he had not.

"I'll make an exception." She quickly changed the subject. "I'm surprised you didn't get Jed to come over. He likes your style."

"Evidently not enough. Why isn't he here now instead of letting you run the risks alone?"

"Oh, he doesn't know I'm here. I told him I was going to Germany to interview East Berliners about life after unification." She made a face. "I figured that sounded boringly safe enough, even for him."

"Instead you come here and try to get yourself killed by terrorists."

"Neither of us is going to get killed." She looked at him uncertainly. "I did a good job so far, didn't I?"

He smiled. "Very good."

She felt a rush of pleasure. "Well, then there's no reason to think the rest of the plan won't go off as well."

"You didn't answer me. Why didn't you want the fantastic Jed with you?"

"He's having a baby."

His lips twitched. "Then he's more fantastic than I deemed possible."

"I told you I wasn't good with words." She grinned. "His wife, Ysabel, is pregnant and he can't think of anything else right now."

"Not even you?"

"He's my friend, not my keeper." She discarded a seven and dealt herself one. "Besides, I wouldn't have asked Jed on this one."

"Why not?"

"It was my business, not—" She stopped when she saw his gaze narrowing on her face. Cripes, she had almost blurted out more than he needed to know. Falkner exuded a rock-firm strength that, combined with an intent concentration, seemed to draw her into making the most intimate confidences. "You're good," she said. "I heard you were a hotshot reporter at one time. Jed's got that same way of listening to people he's interviewing that makes them want to tell him their life stories."

"These days I use the technique only when

I really want to know." He paused. "And the subject is being evasive."

"Me?" She shrugged. "I'm clear as glass. Ask Jed."

"But Jed's not here," he said softly. "And some kinds of glass have ripples that distort and present a vision that's not really true."

She threw back her head and laughed. "I love it! Good God, you make me sound as mysterious as Mata Hari."

"Do I?" His gaze was fixed on the pulse in the hollow of her neck. "God, you have a lovely throat."

Comfort and security vanished, and she suddenly felt as breathless and uncertain as she had when he'd been pressed against her. "I heard Mata Hari did too," she said flippantly. As he continued staring at her with that faint smile, the air in the room seemed to become charged, to press down on her. Her hands were trembling, so that the cards shook. This had to stop. She went on the attack. "Did you know Mora Renord has been playing the heartbroken mistress while you've been a guest here in Said Ababa? She has yellow ribbons wrapped around every tree on the grounds of her Beverly Hills estate."

"Really?" He smiled, his gaze unwavering.

"It doesn't surprise me. Mora has always milked situations for every word of publicity they were worth."

"You don't mind?"

"Why should I? She has her own priorities and I have mine. We always manage to meet on common ground."

"You mean, in a common bed," she said dryly. "And Lynn Cartwright claims you're engaged to her."

His smile vanished. "Now, that I do mind. I don't like lies." He looked up into her eyes. "Any more?"

"What?"

"Aren't you going to drag out any more of my past liaisons as red herrings?"

"I don't know what you mean."

"The hell you don't. The best way to escape a probe is to intercept and then initiate your own. A man's personal life is usually the area most open to attack."

"Not yours." She met his gaze. "You don't let anyone close enough to touch you, do you?"

He stiffened.

She had hit a nerve. It was about time. She was tired of being on the defensive. "Oh, you have plenty of friends, but you've never had a permanent mistress or a wife. I have a theory about that."

"I can't wait to hear it," he said silkily.

"You regard your employees as your family."

"And why do I do that?"

She frowned. "I'm not sure. I'll have to think about it."

"But I'm sure you'll tell me when you come to a conclusion."

"Geez, you don't have to be so testy. You're the one who started this."

"I didn't expect you to—" He broke off and a smile lit his face. "You're right. I shouldn't dish it out if I can't take it. You're proving to be an interesting challenge, Ronnie."

"I'm not trying to be a challenge. I'm just doing a job." She spread her hand out on the bed. "Full house."

He threw down his cards. "You were telling the truth. You're very good"—he paused—"at cards."

She frowned. "Look, I didn't mean to pry into your private life. It just seemed—"

"A good defense?"

She nodded. "You ask too many questions."

"It's the only way to get to know someone."

"I've known Jed for six years and he never asked me anything. He just accepted me as I was."

"Then he has a singular lack of curiosity for a newsman. Perhaps I'd better rethink upping my offer." He stared at her. "All right, I'll try to restrain my curiosity, but there's one more question I want to ask."

"What?" she said warily, not looking him in the eye.

"Nothing very sensitive. I just want to know why you came after me."

"The Emmy. I told you that I—" She broke off as she finally met his gaze. "Oh, all right. I liked your face."

"I beg your pardon?"

"I kept seeing your picture everywhere and it made me feel—" She stopped, searching for words.

"What?" he asked, intrigued.

"Safe."

"Safe?"

She could tell he didn't like the description, but there was nothing she could do about that. It was the truth. She nodded. "I'd never seen anyone who looked as strong and sure of himself as you did. And I'd already heard how you took care of your people and I liked that too."

"Good God."

"What's wrong now? For heaven's sake, you act as if I've insulted you."

"You have a father fixation on me."

She blinked. "Nonsense. I already have a father."

"Oh, yes, this Evan," he said grimly. "Tell me about Evan. When do I meet him?"

"You don't. He's no longer in Said Ababa."

"He left you alone? It appears this father of yours isn't at all protective." His lips tightened. "Well, I'll be damned if I'll take his place. For Lord's sake, I'm only thirty-seven. I'm not ready to adopt a thrill-crazy kid who wants to—"

"Are you nuts? I'm not asking anything of you but that you don't do anything stupid and get us killed." Her voice turned fierce as she went on. "And I'm *not* a kid and Evan is already more father than I can handle. Why should I want another when he's always—"

"Okay. Okay." He grimaced as he held up a hand to stop the barrage of words. "You stung my ego, but I don't have any right to condemn your motives when you've saved my life. I apologize. Can we forget it?"

She couldn't forget it. For some reason the accusation bothered her. "For Pete's sake," she burst out, "there's nothing wrong with liking someone's face."

"Nothing wrong at all," he said wearily. "I suppose I shouldn't complain. No one has liked this ugly mug of mine enough to risk their neck for it before."

What did she really know about Gabe Falkner? Perhaps it had been more than his ego she had hurt. She instinctively rushed on to soothe the wound. "Your face isn't ugly. It's not pretty, but it has . . . character."

"And positively exudes safety. Now that's a word boring enough to please even your Jed."

There didn't seem to be anything she could do to repair the damage. She sighed. "I wish Fatima would get back with our clothes."

"Why? I'm beginning to become accustomed to being nude in your presence. Or don't I present the proper paternal image for you?"

She chose to ignore the goad. "You wouldn't let me shoot you without clothes."

"Shoot?" His gaze went to the pillow hiding the Magnum. "I didn't think our little contretemps was that serious."

"Very funny. You know I mean with my camera. I want to get some pictures while we're here at Fatima's. I haven't taken any footage since you started down the Street of Camels."

His eyes widened. "You were shooting footage just before the escape?"

"Of course. But I had to stop right away. Everything was moving too fast." She shook her head. "Pity."

"I suppose I should be glad you thought my life was worth sacrificing a good picture."

"Don't be silly. I have my priorities straight." She continued wistfully: "Still, it would have been wonderful. All that action . . . Oh, well, I'll get more while we're on the road." She shrugged, then took the camera out of her bag. "And here."

"Not yet," he said. "I prefer to be clothed in more than my dignity before you indulge your passion." He smiled crookedly. "However, if we could come to terms about indulging my own passion, I might be persuaded to give you your way."

She felt color heat her cheeks. "I'll wait."

He repeated her own word softly: "Pity."

The tone of his voice, the attitude of his naked body were suddenly charged with sensuality. She could feel her breasts swell in response beneath the thin cotton sheet draped over them. Cripes, what was wrong with her?

"Come off it," she said gruffly. "I know I hurt your feelings, but you'll get over it. I don't know why men feel that every argument with a woman has to be settled in bed."

"I actually prefer that they be settled before bed, but the other way can be exciting too."

She made a face. "You see, you're like all the rest."

"And just who are the 'rest' of the men in your life?"

The edge was back in his voice, she noticed. "You're not really interested." She made a vague gesture with her hand and changed the subject. "This is a great camera. I've had it for four years and the lenses are—"

"I'm sure your camera is superb and I don't give a damn about your lenses." He forced her to meet his gaze. "I'll let you back away from this confrontation, but I want to make a few things clear. First and foremost, I am not your father and I have no intention of acting like one. Second, I am not in the habit of going to bed with women 'to take the edge off' or to try to win an argument. I've always thought sex was the purest form of pleasure and should be performed with the greatest thought and skill and drive. I haven't had a woman in over a year and I'm horny as hell, but I don't want one of Fatima's women. I'll wait until I can have the partner I do want." He paused. "Shall I tell you what's going to occur when I have that partner?"

She couldn't seem to look away. The intensity in his face was holding her mesmerized. Her heart was beating like thunder.

"A celebration," he said quietly. "One hell of an erotic celebration." He glanced over her head. "Hello, Fatima."

She hadn't heard the door open behind her, but her relief at the interruption was so strong it almost made her dizzy. She jumped to her feet and whirled to face Fatima, who stood in the doorway, her arms piled high with garments. "Oh, clothes. That's great."

"Speak for yourself," Gabe murmured.

"Will you lie down?" Gabe asked impatiently. "You've been striding around the room for the past hour. You're going to wear a hole through those floorboards."

"Evan paid Fatima enough so she can afford to replace them." She continued to pace. "I'm restless."

"Obviously."

"And you won't let me take any more shots of you."

"You've taken enough footage already to paper Radio City Music Hall."

"Well, you never can tell when you're going to lose a cassette. Once in Kuwait I lost an entire camera bag full of film. If I hadn't stashed a few tapes away in another place, I would have been up a creek."

"How did you lose your bag?"

"Iraqi military. They caught me shooting something they didn't want filmed."

"Military emplacements?"

She shook her head. "Torture of civilians."

"My God, were you crazy? Those pictures would have been like a loaded gun pointed at the head of every officer on the squad." He paused. "And there's no way they'd simply let you walk away."

She shrugged. "I was lucky. They just shoved me into prison. The war started a month after that and they kind of forgot about me."

"You're lucky they didn't take you out and shoot you. Where was Jed? Having another baby?"

"Don't be silly. He hadn't met Ysabel then. He was in Washington. He didn't even know I was in Kuwait. I told you I was free-lance. This was *my* job."

"I didn't see any of that film on Jed's program."

"I didn't send them to Jed."

"Why not?"

"That wasn't why I was— Why are you asking me all these questions?"

"Why didn't you send him the film?"

He wasn't going to give up. "Because I sent it to the Human Rights Commission to use as evidence. I was afraid if it appeared on the air, it might lessen the value to the prosecution at a war trial." She burst out, "And I wasn't being noble or soft or quixotic. It just seemed to be the thing to do at the time. Well, maybe a little soft. I'd just gotten out of a Kuwait hospital and I was probably under the weather."

"You don't have to make excuses," Gabe said quietly. "There are times when we all have to make decisions about our priorities."

"But it would have been such a great story." She couldn't help sounding wistful.

"It's still a great story. We just may never see it on television." He leaned back against the headboard. "If you were so lucky, how did you end up in a hospital?"

"Malnutrition. They didn't feed us much during the war." She bit her lower lip. "And I got a little nervous."

"Nervous?"

"I hate being shut up. I get claustrophobic. It's always driven me crazy. I don't know how you stood being a prisoner for a year."

"It's all in the mind-set. After a while it became a game."

She looked at him in wonder. "How could it be? The walls close in on you and the darkness is terrible. There were times when I'd lie there in all that blackness and be afraid I'd smother before morning came."

"You knew you'd react like that and you still took the chance?"

"I thought I'd get away. I did plenty of times before. I almost did that time too." She held up her thumb and index finger. "I was that close."

"And even closer to getting chopped," he said grimly. "For God's sake, stop pacing and come to bed. It's almost three and you're going to need your strength tomorrow."

"I'm not tired. I told you I—" She drew a deep breath. "You're right. I'm not being sensible and I'm keeping you awake. You need your rest."

"Right." He patted the bed. "And so do you."

She lay down on the far side of the bed and curled up into a tight ball. "You can turn off the light now."

"We'll leave it on. The light doesn't bother me."

Relief poured through her. No smothering darkness tonight. Her nerves were stretched so taut she had not known whether she could bear it. "You're not just saying that? I'm almost over it, you know. The doctor said it would take a little while, but that was years ago and now I'm—"

"A chatterbox," he growled. "Don't you ever stop talking?"

"Sorry." She remained quiet a moment. "You're sure it doesn't bother you?"

"The only thing that bothers me is your talking." He rolled over and threw an arm over her body. "Now go to sleep."

She hadn't thought she could be more tense, but she had been wrong. "Why . . . are you doing that?"

"I'll sleep better. There's nothing worse than being alone with your fear."

"You're afraid?"

"I'd be an ass if I wasn't."

She felt the stiffness ease out of her. It was all right to give in, to reach out for comfort if she had something to give in return. She nestled back against him and closed her eyes. "It's going to be okay. You don't have to be afraid. I've planned everything. I've set up a helicopter pickup with your people from the station. They're waiting across the border in Sedikhan for me to radio them that I've got you."

"Oh, you've got me all right."

"I've stashed a radio in a cave in the hills above the Sedikhan border. We'll call for help from there. You should be in safe territory by tomorrow night. Maybe sooner."

"That's comforting." His hand stroked her hair. "This stuff feels like stubby duck feathers."

Nothing could have been less casual than the comment, but his hand stroking her hair was magically soothing. For the first time tonight she felt safe. "I have to keep it short." She yawned. "Long hair isn't practical when you're on a job."

"No, I can see how it might get in the way when you're crawling through those damn pint-sized drainage pipes."

She chuckled. "But you fit, didn't you? And we made it here." Her words sounded slurred even to herself. "Don't be scared. Everything is going to be fine."

"If you ever shut up and let me sleep."

"Sorry. Jed says I'm a motormouth. Did I tell you . . . I don't remember what I was going to say. But sometimes it helps to talk. . . ."

"Shh . . ." His deep voice reverberated in her ear. "I know. But not now, Ronnie."

"No, not now . . ."

THREE

Lord, he hated this damn light.

For six weeks during the first period of his captivity, brilliant lights were kept constantly shining in his face, making sleep impossible. Darkness had become a comfort and a blessing.

But it was no blessing to Ronnie Dalton.

His arms tightened around her slim body. Even though she seemed in the depths of sleep, he could still detect faint signs of tension. She was as wired as a coiled spring ready to explode, but with no preconceived direction. Lord, what a bizarre mixture of brash, funny child and world-weary woman. One moment she was full of toughness and bravado and the next she revealed glimpses of uncertainty and softness. Just when he had thought she was completely honest and open, she drew back within herself and he sensed an odd secret loneliness.

He muttered a curse beneath his breath as his arms tightened protectively around her even more. He hadn't counted on this tenderness barging into his life. In the space of only a few hours she had edged closer to him than he had ever allowed anyone before. She had aroused his body and he could accept that physical reaction, but he hadn't expected to feel this overwhelming sense of possession. She had fallen asleep as trustingly as an orphan child clinging to safety in a dangerous world.

Lord, and now he was supposed to be Daddy Warbucks to her Orphan Annie.

She felt soft and small and completely *woman* in his arms. His body was hardening against her and he drew a deep steadying breath. He had been through more torturous moments than this during the past year, but at the moment he couldn't remember them.

He closed his eyes and shut out that blasted light.

It wouldn't hurt him to be Daddy Warbucks for one night.

But why the hell had no one ever considered how Daddy Warbucks would feel when Annie grew up? There was no natural tie between them and the two had always been more friends than father and daughter. Even if she turned out ugly as sin, there was still all that bravery and character and vulnerability that stirred deeper feelings than beauty ever would.

He was beginning to feel damn sorry for the bastard.

She awoke to find Gabe Falkner sitting quietly in a chair across the room watching her sleep. "What time is it?" She sat up and swung her feet to the floor, casting a hasty glance at the window. Only a pearly light was glowing in the sky, she realized with relief.

"It's a little after six," Gabe said.

She jumped out of bed. "I slept like a log."

"No, you didn't." He stood up and stretched. "You were restless all night. It's surprising you slept at all."

He obviously hadn't done the same. She could sense the charged alertness, the taut awareness that lay beneath that lazy facade.

"I'm used to sleeping in war zones." She moved toward the bathroom. "But then so are you."

"I want out of this particular war zone." His

voice was suddenly layered with repressed violence. "Now."

She grinned at him over her shoulder. "Can you wait until I brush my teeth?"

"Maybe." She could see him relax a little and a faint smile curved his lips. "If you don't floss."

She stopped at the bathroom door. "We'll be out of here in fifteen minutes. You'll have to put the contacts and beard back on. Fatima will bring you a native robe and a burnoose and sunglasses."

"Won't the sunglasses look too much like a disguise?"

"Not in an open Jeep. Everyone wears them in desert country."

"And what role are you playing this time?"

"I'm your driver." She made a face. "Complete with draperies and a smothering veil. You have the easy part."

"A woman driver in a Middle Eastern country?" he asked skeptically.

"Oh, men aren't above teaching women modern skills that will serve their august masculinity," she said. "Women chauffeur men all over Said Ababa." She added, "But, of course, no woman is allowed to drive without a man in the car or written permission from the closest male relative.

That would give her ideas above her station. It's really a charming country."

"I've found it so."

Ronnie remembered the video shot of Gabe bruised and defiant and felt the same surge of anger she had known the first time she had seen it. "This is going to be a piece of cake. I've got forged papers that can't be faulted, if we're stopped. They won't be able to touch you again. I promise, Gabe."

He smiled at her, a warm genuine smile that held neither irony nor sarcasm. "I feel greatly comforted. With such a fierce protector I'm certain I'm as safe as in my own hometown. That being the case"—he made a gesture with his left hand that was both grandiloquent and regal—"you may floss."

"I told you there wouldn't be any trouble." Ronnie pressed on the accelerator and the Jeep picked up speed. "Smooth as oil."

"Oil isn't all that smooth when it gushes out of the ground." Gabe glanced back over his shoulder at the town receding in the distance. "And it tends to be explosive. We're not home free yet. We got through the checkpoint and I don't see any ground pursuit, but the Red December has helicopters."

"They won't be able to spot us once we reach the hills." She jerked off the heavy veil and wig and threw them on the floor. "Lord, those things are hot. You wonder how the Said Ababan men manage to survive those veils."

He lifted his brows. "It's the women who wear them."

"But it's the men who make the women wear them. You can bet if I had to spend more than twenty-four hours in one, I'd go gunning for the male chauvinist who put it on me."

"Dear me, how savage," he murmured. "Have you considered that it may only be our poor male chauvinists' insecurity that makes us veil our women from other men?"

"That's their problem." She shot him a glance. "And you shouldn't include yourself in that lot. You're not a chauvinist or you wouldn't send women reporters into war zones."

"I have my protective moments, but I try to fight them." He smiled. "For instance, at the moment I'm fighting the impulse to tell you to put on that veil again."

She stiffened. "You are?"

"Don't get bent out of shape. I merely think

you should cover your head before this desert sun takes its toll."

"Oh!" She picked up the veil and draped it over her head. "I didn't think. You're right."

He looked at her in surprise.

"Well, I may be independent, but I'm not an idiot," she said in answer to his unspoken question. "Recovering from sunstroke isn't what I have planned for the next few months."

"What do you have planned?"

"I don't know. Yugoslavia maybe."

She saw him stiffen. "Why doesn't that surprise me? You do know snipers are still shooting newspeople over there."

"I make a small target." She grinned. "And I'll leave my bull's-eye sweatshirt at home."

"Very funny." He didn't sound amused. "Why don't you give it a rest for a few months . . . providing you get out of here without being shot."

She shook her head. "I get restless."

"So you go looking for guerrillas to shoot at you."

He sounded definitely uptight. "No, I go looking for pictures to take," she corrected. "And Yugoslavia should provide some dandy opportunities."

"I don't doubt it. With any luck you'll find

yourself tossed in a secret concentration camp or raped or taken—"

"Luck goes in cycles," she interrupted. "I figure I've had my bad luck for the next five years."

"Yeah, sure," he muttered.

"Geez, what are you beefing about? You've had your own Yugoslavias and I'm not one of your people."

"Aren't you?" He gave her a glance of exasperation and frustration. "I think you're very much mine."

Possessiveness. She felt a strange breathlessness that had nothing to do with the desert sun. She had known he was possessive, but it felt odd being sheltered under that umbrella herself. "You forget I'm strictly free-lance. I have no intention of hooking up with your network."

"Why not? I can offer you excellent money and unlimited opportunities."

She shrugged. "I'm free-lance," she repeated. "I like it that way."

"And I don't," he said flatly. "At least, if I was your boss, I could monitor your movements and know what the hell you were up to."

She shook her head.

"Dammit, take the job."

"Dammit, I won't. I know you're grateful to

me, but you don't have to do anything to show it." She added lightly, "I'll have my Emmy."

"So you're just going to walk away."

"No, *you're* going to *fly* away. Once we reach Sedikhan, I'll go my way and you'll go yours."

"I don't like that scenario."

"Too bad," she said. She was silent a moment and then burst out, "Look, you don't have to pay me back. I owed you. Now we're even, okay?"

"You owed me?"

She nodded. "And now we're even, so stop worrying about it."

"And what did I do to incur this debt?"

"Never mind." She shot him a sly glance. "Maybe you were my inspiration. Pygmalion to my Galatea."

"First Daddy Warbucks and now Pygmalion," he muttered. "And I don't believe a word of that crap."

"That's your choice."

"Why do you owe me?"

She didn't answer.

"I'm going to find out, you know," he said softly. "I'm not going to stop until I do."

And Gabe Falkner's determination was legendary. She had made a mistake. She should have left it alone, but she had been afraid his sense of obligation would be stronger than his curiosity. "We'll see. You'll probably forget all about it when you get back to the States."

"I won't forget. Not about Said Ababa and not about you." He paused. "You definitely top my list of unforgettable people."

He topped her list of unforgettable people also. She suddenly knew she had wanted him to be less than the larger-than-life man she had studied all these years. Maybe the reason she had been so determined to free him was that she, too, had wanted to be released from bondage. Instead she was finding herself drawn even tighter, closer.

"I'm flattered, but that would be pretty stupid of you. You'll have to work on it. There's no sense dwelling on people who are no longer in your life." She pointed to the hills in the distance. "You see that hill with the bald top? There's a small plateau just behind it where a helicopter can land. We'll set up camp, radio your people in Sedikhan, and then wait for the helicopter."

"Oh, will we?"

That hadn't pleased him either. She sighed. "Cripes, what do you want me to do? Put on that blasted veil again and meekly let you handle everything? It's a good plan."

He suddenly smiled. "I know it is. Sorry, you ruffled my feathers again."

His smile was warm and as rare as the man himself, and she felt a sudden despair. It was hard to keep a distance from a man who could admit he was wrong. How the devil was she going to forget the bastard, if he kept showing her facets of himself she found appealing?

"Well, I guess your feathers aren't as easily ruffled as some I've run across. I suppose I'll forgive you."

His smile deepened with amusement. "I'm most gratified."

Ronnie looked up from the fire she was building as Gabe turned off the radio. "Who's John?"

Gabe strolled over, then dropped down on the ground on the other side of the fire. "John Grant."

"Have you been together a long time? He was all choked up."

"Seven years. He was the producer of my first television news show. He's executive vice-president now." He swallowed. "And I'm pretty choked up myself. I wasn't sure if I'd ever see him again."

No macho denial of emotion. She liked that. Dammit, she was afraid she was beginning to like everything about him. "When I set up the pickup, I talked to a Daniel Bredlowe."

"Dan is my executive assistant."

"They like you." She made a face. "Of course, it's easier to like a boss who's cooped up in a prison than underfoot all the time."

"True, but I really think they don't actually detest me even when I'm around. Of course, I could be wrong."

The fire was burning brightly now and she sat back on her heels. "No, they jumped on the chance of getting you out. Bredlowe even offered to come with me."

"You should have let him. Dan's good in a tight corner."

She giggled as a thought occurred to her. "But where would we have put him in the bordello? Under the bed?"

"Certainly not in it." His voice was suddenly thick. "There wasn't room for anyone between us."

Her cheeks flamed as she remembered him pressed against her, her legs clinging to his naked hips. "No, there wasn't." She looked away from him. "I didn't want outside interference. Evan was nervous as it was." She stirred the fire. "The helicopter won't get here for an hour or so. My instructions were not to come until full dark. If you like, I could make some coffee."

"Not unless you want some. I'm too wired for caffeine at the moment. I have enough adrenaline running in my veins to run the generator at Hoover Dam."

He didn't look wired. His big body was sprawled catlike on the ground, his head resting on his hand, his gaze fixed intently on her face.

The silence grew and her tension with it. "I've never been to Hoover Dam. It's in Arizona, isn't it?"

He nodded.

"I try to see at least one national treasure whenever I'm in the States. I went to Yosemite last time and a year ago I did Washington, D.C. Have you ever gone to see the Declaration of Independence?"

"Of course."

"There's no 'of course' about it. The guide told me that it wasn't one of the most popular things to see anymore." She shook her head. "I don't understand it. You'd think they'd all want to see it."

'They?'

"Citizens," she said with impatience. "You know, 'we the people.'"

He smiled faintly. "Oh, that 'they.'"

"They don't know what they've got."

"But you know?"

"You bet I do," she said. "I learned it in a dozen countries that never saw a constitution or a bill of rights. Lord, they're lucky."

"Aren't you using the wrong pronoun?"

She had made a mistake and rushed to cover it. "*We're* lucky," she corrected. "I guess I spend so much time out of the country, my viewpoint is a little remote."

"You didn't sound remote. You sounded passionate as hell."

She considered it better not to answer. Silence again fell between them.

"I wish you wouldn't stare at me," she finally burst out. "I feel like a bug under a microscope."

"You're certainly a very rare species," he said. "And I have to admit I find you a fascinating study."

"I don't know why. I'm pretty ordinary." She amended quickly, "Except for my work; that's exceptional." She reached into the leather bag on the ground next to her, turned on the camcorder, and focused on him.

"The freed captive at ease," she murmured.

"Shut that damn thing off."

"Oh, all right." She turned off the camcorder and set it down. "I'll wait until the helicopter comes and get a shot of you flying off into the sunset."

"Moonlight." Then the full impact of her words hit home and he slowly sat up. "What the hell do you mean? How can you take a shot of me flying off if you're in the helicopter?"

"But I won't be in it," she said. "We part company here. I'm driving the Jeep to Sedikhan."

"The devil you are. That helicopter will be at Marasef airport within thirty minutes of takeoff. You said yourself it wasn't safe to take the road to the border."

"That was only because you were along."

"You're a journalist too. What do you think will happen if you get stopped at the border?"

"I'll try to slide over without them seeing me, but even if they find out who I am ..." She shrugged. "I'm small potatoes and they're looking for a big fish."

"Sounds like a smorgasbord," he said caustically. "But I have a hunch you'd be the main course. Now, tell me what reason you could possibly have for going by road."

She looked into the fire. "Why should I leave a perfectly good Jeep here to rot?"

"I'll pay for the damn Jeep."

"Why should you? I can just as well drive it across—"

"You go one step near that Jeep and I'll tear out the motor and scatter the parts from here to the Mediterranean."

She set her jaw. "Then I'll walk across the border."

He stared at her. "Lord, and you'd be stubborn enough to do it." He struggled with his temper for a moment and then said quietly, "You may be stubborn, but you're not stupid. What's the real reason you don't want to go with me in that helicopter?"

She didn't answer him.

"If you don't tell me, I'm going to send the helicopter back to Marasef and we'll both drive to the border."

"You can't do that," she said.

"Try me."

Her hands clenched into fists. "You're going to spoil everything. Do you want to end up a prisoner again?"

"No, and I don't want you to, either."

She wasn't going to be able to sway him so she gave in. "There will be too much coverage."

His eyes widened. "I beg your pardon?"

"Your helicopter will probably be met in Marasef by half the reporters in the Middle East and the CIA and—"

"What difference does that make? You're a reporter yourself."

"It's very different," she said fiercely. "No one pays any attention to just one reporter on a news crew, but you'd be in the spotlight and some of it would be bound to spill over onto me. I can't have that."

"Why the hell not?"

"I have my reasons."

"None that are worth your life."

"That's my decision to make," she said. "And if you really think you owe me something, you can pay me back by getting on that helicopter tonight and stop trying to mess up my life."

"How the devil would I be—" He broke off as he met her blazing eyes. His lips tightened. "Okay, I'll take the helicopter."

"And you won't nag me to go along?" she persisted.

"Why should I waste my time?" He got up and turned away. "I give you my solemn promise I'll not make the slightest damn attempt to nag you to save your own neck."

FOUR

The helicopter hovered and then landed with a soft thud on the grassy plateau.

"Come on." Ronnie grabbed Gabe's arm and started running toward the aircraft. "We have to get you out of here. Those lights can be seen for miles."

Gabe's long legs were easily outdistancing hers. "Leaving you right on ground zero," he muttered savagely.

"The sooner you take off, the sooner I'll be on my way too."

The door of the helicopter was opening and a slim, wiry man wearing a leather flight jacket jumped down.

"Bredlowe?" she asked as she came within calling distance.

"Right."

She reached into her bag, drew out her camcorder, and told Gabe, "You go ahead. I want to catch a shot of you two together."

"Why doesn't that surprise me?" Nevertheless he sprinted forward and grasped the man's hand.

Bredlowe's eyes were glistening in the lights of the helicopter as he said something to Gabe. She couldn't hear over the roar of the rotors, but there was no mistaking either the emotion or the drama of the greeting between the two men.

Gabe turned to her. "Put the camera down and come meet my friends." His voice was gruff and his eyes as moist as Bredlowe's. She reluctantly switched off the camera and hurried forward. It was great stuff, but she had enough footage and Gabe needed to get under way.

"Dan Bredlowe, Ronnie Dalton," Gabe said. "Ronnie tells me you've already met by phone."

Bredlowe's hand enveloped Ronnie's. "Lord, I didn't think you could pull it off. You're a bloody miracle."

At closer range he looked to be in his late twenties, with a shock of curly brown hair and hazel eyes that gazed at her as if she were Mother Teresa and Michelle Pfeiffer rolled into one. It made her uncomfortable. "Hi," she said awkwardly. "You'd better get him out of here." She turned to Gabe and thrust out her hand. "It's time for you to go. Good-bye."

He took her hand and warmth flowed through her as it had the first time he had touched her.

He was staring at her, his face impassive, but she could sense the storm of emotion in him. He didn't like this. Well, she didn't either, but she didn't have a choice.

"Oh, will you do me a favor?" She withdrew her hand, opened her camera, and took out the cassette. "Will you keep this for me? I'll send for it as soon as I'm safe."

"So you won't get caught with it?" he asked caustically.

"I won't get caught. It's just safe practice to guard the story. Will you?"

He took the cassette and jammed it into his jacket pocket. "Come with me."

She shook her head, a tremulous smile on her lips. "Not possible. And you promised not to nag me."

"I won't nag you." He gestured to the pilot in the plane. "This is David Carroll, my pilot."

She turned her head to see the brown-skinned pilot, his wide smile gleaming in the lighted dash of the cockpit as he leaned forward to offer his hand.

"A pleasure," he said softly.

"Nice to meet—"

Pain exploded in her jaw!

Blackness followed.

Dan gasped. "Gabe, what the hell are you—"

"Grab that camera," Gabe rapped as he caught Ronnie's slumping body. "She'll castrate me if anything happens to it."

Dan grabbed the camera as it fell from Ronnie's lax fingers. "She might do it anyway. A right to the jaw isn't the way most people show gratitude for saving their lives."

"It was that or let her risk her neck again trying to reach the border." He carried Ronnie to the helicopter, settled her in one of the backseats, and fastened her seat belt. "No way was I going to let that happen. Let's get the hell out of here, Dave."

The pilot watched him climb into the seat beside Ronnie and fasten his seat belt. "Is she okay? She's out like a light."

"You hit her pretty hard," Dan accused.

"Shut up and get in the helicopter," Gabe said through his teeth. He was feeling enough guilt; he didn't need any more heaped on him.

Dan jumped into the helicopter, taking the other front seat, and slammed the door. "Take off, Dave." As the helicopter became airborne he turned back to look at Gabe. "I suppose you had a reason for this. Why didn't she want to come with us?"

"Something about not wanting to be in the limelight." He gently tilted Ronnie's head so it lay more comfortably on the headrest. The bruise was already showing on that exquisite peaches-and-cream skin. He felt like one of those creeps who battered women. When she woke up he'd be lucky if she didn't use that .357 Magnum on him. Hell, maybe he'd let her. "How bad is the reception committee going to be at Marasef airport?"

"There will be our own reporters, of course." Dan made a face. "And we had no choice but to tell the CIA you'd been released so they could pull their men out of the danger zone. That means there will probably be leaks to other news services."

"So we can expect a media circus."

"But with our own network in the center ring," Dan said quickly. "And once the officials whisk you away to Frankfurt for medical tests, we'll be the only ones permitted to—"

"No Frankfurt."

"You know all hostages go to the hospital there for medical assessment."

"That doesn't mean I have to go." He turned back to Ronnie. She looked as fragile and break-able as one of the porcelain dolls in his aunt's collection.

I'm not going to let you mess up my life.

Ronnie had known the risks of staying, but she had been willing to take them for reasons of her own. He had not been able to leave her, but he had no right to judge the consequences of her plan of action when he was ignorant of the nature of those risks.

He leaned forward and spoke to David. "Change direction. Head south, we're not going to Marasef airport."

She was being carried down a gleaming ivory-and-gold tile hallway, passing magnificent paint-ings, priceless panels with intricate frets . . .

"A museum?" she muttered. "What the devil am I doing in a museum?"

"Not a museum. A palace," Gabe said. "Open the door, Dan."

A palace?

Gabe strode into a chamber as magnificent as the corridor through which she had been carried. "Thanks, Dan. Now get out of here before the fireworks start."

"Gladly," Dan said. "See you later."

She was being placed on something silken and cushioned, a chaise longue. Then Gabe was gone.

A moment later an ice pack settled against her jaw. She flinched, her eyes focusing on Gabe's face a few inches from her own.

"Easy," he said quietly. "Let me hold it here. The ice will bring the swelling down."

"Why should I have—" Her eyes widened in realization and outrage. "You hit me!"

"How else was I to—" He gasped when her fist connected with his stomach and the breath left him.

She jumped to her feet, glaring at him. "Damn you!"

He straightened painfully. "At least you didn't use the gun."

"I should have," she said with ferocity. "You deserve it. What gave you the right to interfere? I told you I couldn't come with you to—"

"Hold it!" he interrupted. "I agree I deserve

any reasonable punishment you care to dish out. Do you want to hit me again? I won't even put up a fight."

Her hands slowly unclenched. "You shouldn't have done it. You had no right."

"And you had no right to put me in a position where I felt helpless to do anything else. Do you think I like beating up on women?"

"How do I know?" She gingerly touched her jaw. "You certainly hit me hard enough."

"I had to knock you out." He grimaced. "But I had no idea you had the proverbial glass jaw. I thought you'd wake up in the helicopter."

"You shouldn't have done it," she repeated. She looked around the huge room. The decor was a cross between Mediterranean and elegant French Provincial. The couch was pure turquoise-cushioned opulence, the floor white marble tile covered by a delicate cream-and-blue Aubusson carpet, and the French doors might have graced a harem in ancient days. "Is this a hotel?"

He shook his head. "The palace."

She vaguely remembered him saying something about one. "What palace?"

"The royal palace of Sedikhan. You seemed so adamant about avoiding the spotlight, I had Dave land us on the palace grounds instead of the airport. I radioed ahead and got permission from Sheikh Ben Raschid, the reigning head of state, and he'll run interference for us until we get our bearings."

A flare of hope shot through her. She might be able to salvage this disaster yet. "Then nobody knows I'm here?"

"Not yet." He paused. "But I'm not going to lie to you. We had to tell the authorities I'm here and Dan said your name was mentioned to the CIA as the instigator of the rescue attempt."

"Damn, they might as well have broadcast it by satellite." She drew a long breath, trying to think. "It may still be okay. I can take off right away. If I'm not here, they can't ask questions." She looked around the suite. "Where's my camera bag?"

"Still in the helicopter," he said. "And there's no sense you running away yet. I don't deny there will be leaks, but no one is going to be able to reach you while you're here."

He made it sound so easy. He didn't realize her only chance was to get away before— She was lying to herself, she realized. It was already too late.

"That won't help," she said dully. "They have

my name and they'll start to dig. You should have left me in Said Ababa."

"It's done. You're here now. Stop bellyaching."

She blinked and then said reluctantly, "You're right, no use crying over spilled milk. I'll just have to clean it up."

"No, I'll clean it up," he said. "But I have to know how much damage control is needed. Why are you so afraid of—"

"It's my business," she said. "Stay out of it."

"Not likely. I brought you here and I'm not—" He stopped as he saw her set expression. "Okay, I'll drop it for now. You could use a good night's sleep and so could I."

She glanced at the king-size bed across the room that was draped with gauze curtains. She had a sudden memory of the chipped headboard of the bed they had shared last night at Fatima's.

As if he had read her mind he said softly, "You can't say I don't provide better for you than you did for me."

She felt a surge of heat. He had not mentioned leaving her. Did he mean to share this suite and that bed with her tonight? Her gaze flew back to his face and she saw him shake his head.

"I'll find my own bunk. I need to get some sleep myself."

The emotion that cascaded through her was a confused rush of relief and disappointment. She tried to make her tone casual. "I didn't think anything else."

"Yes, you did, and so did I. It was as disturbing as hell." He turned away and walked toward the door. "I'll join you here for breakfast at ten and we'll talk."

"I get up early. Six at the latest."

"Then cultivate the luxury life until I get here. Right now I have to go pay my respects to His Majesty and ask a few favors. But tomorrow I'm going to put a hell of a lot of questions to you and I'm going to get some answers."

She scowled. "Maybe."

"Answers," he repeated.

"What would you do if I told you to go jump in the lake to find your blasted answers?" She lifted her chin. "Punch me out again?"

His compelling gaze met her own. "No, but I'll find another way to get them."

Lord, he was determined, she thought with a shiver of apprehension as she watched the door close behind him.

Well, so what? She had fought determined men before and come out on top.

But she didn't want to fight Gabe Falkner. She respected him and admired him and—

She pulled back sharply before she could complete the thought and moved forward to the French doors. She stared out at a lovely courtyard that was crowned by a mosaic-tiled fountain illuminated by strategically placed lights. This place was a vision of peace and beauty, a balm to her frazzled nerves after those weeks in Said Ababa. She should really go find her camera and get out of here, but she knew she wasn't going to do it. It would do no harm to stay in this lovely place for a night. She could leave in the morning. She was tired and needed a bath and—

None of that mattered. They were all excuses. The truth was that she couldn't bear to break from Gabe Falkner with this discord between them. He had been part of her life too long. She wanted the separation to be clean and without anger.

"It's about time you got here," she said as Gabe walked into the suite at eleven the next day. "I hate people who aren't prompt. I've been up since six and prowling around in this— You look terrible. What's wrong with you?"

"Nothing. I'm just a little tired. I couldn't sleep last night. I guess I'm suffering from aftershock." He made a face. "I never thought it could happen to me. I'm not exactly the sensitive type."

But he was sensitive in his relations with others, she wanted to say. He seemed to possess a sixth sense, an empathy she had seen in few men. She felt a surge of sympathy mixed with guilt. He was so tough outwardly she had almost forgotten the ordeal he had just gone through.

"Well, what are you doing standing there?" she asked. "Sit down and eat something." She settled herself at the table the servants had rolled into the suite over an hour ago, uncovered the warming dishes, and spooned eggs and bacon on a plate. "Protein, that's what you need. Energy food. When I was held in Kuwait, I used to get this terrible hunger for bacon. Sometimes I thought I could smell it. What did you get a yen for?"

"Well, I have to admit my primary yen wasn't for food." He went on immediately, "Big Macs." He started to eat the eggs. "I'm a fast-food junkie. I acquired the taste when I became a correspondent. There was almost always a McDonald's in any country I visited. It was like a little piece of home, as American as apple pie."

"Yeah," she said wistfully. "I guess it is."

His gaze raked her face. "That bruise is still pretty evident."

She shrugged. "I've had worse." Grinning, she added, "And given worse."

His hand went to his stomach. "You did last night. Do you want to see my bruise?"

Powerful shoulders gleaming in the lamplight, muscles rippling in a washboard-firm abdomen.

"I don't believe that's necessary." Her hand was trembling a little as she poured coffee into his cup and then her own. "I know my own power."

"I don't think you do." His gaze was fixed thoughtfully on her face. "You pack a punch that doesn't show up on the anatomy." He suddenly chuckled. "Or not in the usual places."

He was speaking of arousal, sexual response. She was used to much more graphic terms and yet she could feel the heat in her cheeks. "I think you need to get home to Mora Renord. Have you called her yet? I'm sure she'd come flying to your bed."

"To 'take the edge off'? I told you I don't use women." He leaned back in his chair. "And I don't want Mora here."

The explosive satisfaction that tore through her was a shock. She looked down at her coffee cup. "Why not?"

"Maybe I prefer Orphan Annie."

She looked up in confusion. "What?" She caught her breath as she met his gaze. "Me?"

"Oh, yes," he murmured. "Most certainly you."

He wanted her. It probably stemmed from propinquity and the provocativeness of their situation last night, but it hadn't ended at Fatima's. He still wanted to go to bed with her. She could feel the swelling of her breasts, the same tingling between her thighs she had experienced in that bed at the bordello.

"Well, aren't you going to say anything?" he asked softly.

"Sure." She lifted her cup to her lips. "You're probably so horny that Godzilla would look good to you, and I'm not Orphan Annie."

He chuckled. "And you're not Godzilla either."

"Nope." She shrugged, feigning casualness. "But I have no intention of crawling into your bed to assuage a year of sexual drought." She sipped her coffee. "I only stuck around to say good-bye. After breakfast I'm on the road."

His smile vanished. "No way."

She ignored his words. "It's been an experience I won't forget. I hope everything goes well for you. Oh, and I'll need my camera and that cassette I gave you."

"You couldn't forget that," he said, acid in his voice. "Shut the door and walk away, but remember the camera."

"It's all I have," she said simply.

The grimness was wiped from his face. "Lord, what am I supposed to say to that?"

"Nothing. Just give me my camera."

He slowly shook his head. "I'd be a fool to do that. I obviously have a valuable hostage. That camera is almost a person to you. I'll trade you."

"For what?" she asked warily.

"Information. I'll give you your camera if you tell me what you're afraid of."

"No deal. I'll get another camera."

"But not like this one. It's been with you for such a long time, it's become almost a part of you."

He was right. She had saved for over a year for the money to buy that camera, and she loved it. "You bastard."

"Tell me," he coaxed. "What do I have to say to convince you that I won't betray you? For

Lord's sake, don't you see I want to help you?"

"You can't help me. You blew it when you brought me here."

"Then I'll put it back together. What the hell do you think I'll do? I'm not going to hurt you, Ronnie."

He couldn't help her either, and she had never told anyone, not even Jed. She should keep her silence. She felt a surge of frustration at the thought. Lord, she was weary of that silence, of not being able to share.

"Ronnie?"

"I don't have a passport," she suddenly found herself saying.

"Is that all?" His expression cleared. "Did you leave it in Said Ababa? No problem. We'll get you a replacement. All we have to do is report the one you lost."

"That's not it. I didn't lose my passport. I still have it. It's just—" She stopped, then blurted out, "It's a phony."

He stiffened. "Phony?"

"You heard me. I bought it on the black market. It's a damn good one, but if anyone started delving, they'd find out it was a phony." She stood up and started pacing. "How am I going to get back to the States? I'm a journalist, for heaven's sake, I need to go where the stories are. I suppose I could buy another passport under another name to use outside the country, but they'd alert U.S. Immigration and I'd never be able to—"

"Wait a minute," Gabe interrupted. "Back up. Why did you have to buy a passport to begin with? Why didn't you just apply for one?"

"Because I'm not an American citizen," she said jerkily. "My father was a naturalized American citizen. When he was convicted of arms running and lying on his citizenship application regarding the crime, he was deported and stripped of his citizenship before I was born."

"I see," he said. "And you're being tarred for your father's sins."

"Not entirely." Her smile was without mirth. "I was picked up by government agents in El Salvador for acting as a lookout for Evan. He managed to get me away from them, but that makes me a criminal too."

"And how old were you when you committed this heinous crime?"

"Eleven. Evan started using me for a lookout when I was eight. No one ever suspects kids." She gave him a sober look. "And it *was* a heinous crime. Evan says he only supplies a demand that would be met by someone else anyway, but I've never fooled myself. Wars can't be fought without guns. You have to be responsible for your own morals and not worry about someone else's."

"You only did what your father told you to do," he said roughly. "You were only a kid, for God's sake."

"I dug in and told him I wouldn't do it any longer when I was fifteen, but it was too late. It's not going to make any difference to Immigration how old I was. I have a criminal record and the United States doesn't want undesirables like me in the country. Like father, like daughter." She tried to smile as she shrugged. "It's all in how you're perceived in this black-and-white world. Immigration doesn't recognize any grays."

"You're not gray, dammit. You're as—" He stopped and then said, "I take it you're afraid the media is going to unearth your unsavory past."

"You know they will. Within two weeks they'll know everything about me down to the number of fillings in my teeth. Your release is the biggest story of the year and it's going to start a press feeding frenzy. You'd read the riot act to any of your journalists who didn't search out every kernel of a story."

"My reporters don't go in for yellow journalism."

"You only say that because you're feeling guilty that you goofed in bringing me here. The truth isn't out of bounds to any reporter and it's not yellow journalism. I'd go after every detail of your story myself. It's only good reporting and—"

"All right, I'll grant you all that's true and I've put you in a rotten position. What's your solution?"

"I'll lie low and stay away from the U.S. Jed will give me assignments."

"In Yugoslavia, no doubt."

"Maybe."

"The hell he will," Gabe said violently. He pushed back his chair. "I'll think of something else."

"Like what?" She shook her head. "Do you think I haven't tried to think of another way out?" She swallowed. "I *liked* pretending I was an American. I felt . . . I liked it."

"If you're not American, what nationality are you?"

She shook her head. "My father thought my mother was Swedish, but he wasn't sure."

"Why the devil didn't he find out?"

"They both lived on the fringe." She smiled bitterly. "You don't know what it's like. You come together for a while and then you drift apart. You travel from country to country and never settle, never belong anywhere. You're the person your passport says you are, and when the passport becomes obsolete, your identity is too. Then you get a new passport and become someone else."

"Lord, what a hell of a life for a kid."

"You get used to it."

"Sure you do."

"You do. You just have to take one day at a time, enjoy every pleasure that comes your way, and ignore all the rest."

"I'd make a bet there were a lot of things you couldn't ignore."

"Some." She grimaced. "For Pete's sake, stop making me out to be a martyr. I had plenty to eat and a bed most of the time. You know, I could have been born in a place like Somalia."

"At least you would have had a country, an advantage that your delightful father didn't provide you."

"He wasn't delightful and you couldn't call him much of a father, but he wasn't a monster either," she said defensively. "Sometimes he was even . . ." She searched for a word for Evan that was not derogatory. "Fun. He never actually—"

"Be quiet and let me think." He stood there, a frown wrinkling his brow as he mentally went over possibilities. "There's just got to be some means to—" He snapped his fingers. "We'll get married."

She stared at him in shock. Marriage to Gabe. A multitude of unidentifiable emotions surged through her in the space of a heartbeat. Then she snapped her own fingers. 'We'll get married,' she mimicked. "That's the dumbest idea I've ever heard. What do you think this is? The movie set of *Pretty Woman*? This is real life. Immigration has had too much experience with phony marriages to acquire citizenship." Her voice was suddenly shaking with intensity. "I want American citizenship more than anything in this world. If it were that simple, I'd have paid some expatriate American to marry me years ago."

His gaze narrowed absently on the painting on the wall across the room. "So we'll have to convince them it's not phony, or at least convince the public. If we can get enough popular support, any political pressure I can apply will be more effective."

She shook her head. "It would never work."

"I can make it work. I'm the man of the hour and you saved my life."

"And if I marry you, it will make me look like an adventuress taking advantage of a man who's been cooped up so long he's lost his judgment."

He smiled. "There's nothing wrong with my judgment."

She wanted to reach out and touch him, listen to him, let him convince her.

"Come on," he challenged. "Let me take a stab at it. What can it hurt? If I don't pull it off, you can still vanish into the mist."

"Mist disappears in the sunlight."

"Put yourself into my hands," he said softly. "I want to do this, Ronnie."

"Why?" she whispered. "I told you that you didn't owe me anything. All debts are paid."

"Ah, that mysterious debt. I can't believe something I can't remember would be worth taking the risks you ran." He gently touched her cheek. "And that isn't why I want to help you."

"Then why?"

His eyes were suddenly twinkling. "Purely selfish. It will give me a better chance of getting you into bed. We've already discussed how horny I am."

"Not that horny."

"You have no idea. And there's also the concept of righting wrongs and setting a terrible criminal on the road to redemption."

"Stop joking. This is serious."

His smile faded. "No one could be more serious than I am at the moment. You helped me out of that hellhole and I want to give you something you value as much as I do my freedom." He held out his hand. "Let me help you, Ronnie."

He was so confident he could mend everything for her, but she knew his efforts would be completely useless. They'd never convince anyone it was a genuine marriage. No one knew better how cynical the world could be. It would be a great risk; she had a lot to lose. Her life was going along quite satisfactorily and those wistful dreams she had held since childhood weren't worth sending it crashing down about her. She didn't really need a country. She should be content with what she had.

But she wasn't content. She had never been content. She *wanted* what he offered her. What if there were risks? she thought recklessly. She had lived on the edge since the day she was born and this gamble was for a prize she had wanted all her life. If she didn't win, she would still have had a few more weeks with this man who had intrigued and fascinated her for the last ten years.

She slowly reached out and put her hand in his.

"Set up a press conference for one o'clock tomorrow afternoon," Gabe said to Dan as he strode into his suite fifteen minutes later. "I want full coverage."

"Our exclusive?" Dan asked as he started for the phone on the desk.

"No, everyone. CBS, ABC, CNN . . ." Gabe picked up the extension on the end table by the couch, accessed the second line, and placed a call to Senator Koras in Washington. "Newspapers too. Everyone." He spoke to Koras's secretary and then, when he was put on hold, added to Dan, "And I want a report on Evan and Ronnie Dalton. Everything derogatory, everything good, and everything in between. I want it by the news conference tomorrow."

Dan gave a low whistle. "That's not going to be easy. Can we count on Ronnie for help?"

Gabe shook his head. "Do it on your own. She's not going to say anything that would incriminate her father even to help herself. She still has a certain amount of loyalty to the scumbag."

"My, how violent we are." Dan picked up the phone. "It's common to have a certain affection for one's parents."

"Not if they don't deserve it. Not if they use you and—" Gabe broke off and tried to control his temper. The thought of Evan Dalton and the life he had made Ronnie lead infuriated him. What the hell was wrong with him? He didn't usually view people so judgmentally, but the idea of Dalton using a kid to— No, not just any kid. Ronnie. The crux of his anger was that Dalton had used Ronnie, who was honest and loyal and beneath that tough veneer more vulnerable than anyone he had ever known.

He had a sudden memory of her sitting by the fire, her expression earnest and a little wistful as she talked about going to see the Declaration of Independence. He couldn't imagine a life without roots or any stability. It was a wonder she had survived to become the unique woman he had met two days ago. Two days? Lord, it seemed a lifetime. He had run the entire gamut of emotions with Ronnie Dalton; lust, respect, amusement, exasperation, possessiveness, pity . . .

The senator came on the line and Gabe spoke quickly. "Yes, I'm fine, Harry. I just called to thank you for your efforts on my behalf. I understand from Dan you were at the president's throat from the time the negotiations to get me back started." He cut off Koras's modest protestation in midsentence. "Yes, you were. That's why I have another favor to ask of you now."

"I don't like this." Ronnie jammed her hands into the pockets of her leather jacket as she walked beside Gabe down the corridor. "Why do I have to be here?"

"Because you're the heroine of the hour," Gabe said placidly. "Why are you so nervous? You've attended hundreds of these news conferences."

"But I was the one asking questions and taking pictures."

"I'll fend off the questions and you'll photograph very well."

"I don't want to be photographed," she said. "I'm surprised you didn't want to send me to Elizabeth Arden and get me up in a haute couture outfit."

"I don't think Sedikhan has an Elizabeth

Arden's and you're fine as you are." His apprais-
ing gaze ran over her casual jeans and chambray
shirt topped by her worn leather jacket. "Fresh
angel's face, attitude a little tough, but that's
okay. You couldn't have pulled off my rescue
if you didn't have those characteristics. It just
makes you appear more interesting."

"Thanks," she said wryly. She moistened her
dry lips. "This is a terrible idea. It's not going to
work, you know."

"If it doesn't, we'll try something else." He
stopped outside the closed door of the conference room and paused. "Listen, Ronnie, I know
this isn't going to be easy for you, but I'll be there
with you all the way." His voice deepened. "I
won't let anyone or anything hurt you again."

His gaze held hers with a forcefulness that
was like a wall of strength. She felt again that
sense of bonding. "Sometimes you can't help
people from getting hurt," she said unsteadily. "It
just . . . happens. I won't blame you if it does."

"I'd blame myself," he said quietly. "I'd blame
myself so much I don't think I could stand it."
His fingers touched her lips. "So I can't let it
happen, can I?"

Her lips felt soft, exquisitely sensitive beneath
his fingers. If she spoke, the words would be

a caress, and she must not permit herself that intimacy.

His mouth suddenly curved with humor as his hand fell away from her. "But do me a favor?"

She would do anything for him at that moment, fight a dragon, blow up CNN's satellite. "What?" she whispered.

"Don't tell the entire world I slugged you."

FIVE

It hadn't been too bad so far, Ronnie thought as her gaze swept over the sea of reporters and cameras. There was James Ketrick, who had been with ABC in Kuwait. She recognized a few other faces. Damn, she wished she was out there with them instead of here on this blasted podium.

The news conference had gone on for over an hour and focused almost entirely on Gabe's experiences during his captivity. Whenever questions came up concerning her part in his escape, he had deftly changed the subject or deflected the question with a promise to address it later. With any luck she'd be able to scoot out of this with a minimum of attention and get—

"And now that we've gone over all the depressing details, we'll move to the more colorful aspects of the story." Gabe leaned forward into

the microphones on the podium. "Dan has prepared a news release to give you all regarding the
exact details of my escape, and I'm sure you've
already heard rumors of my colleague's part in
it." Ronnie stiffened as he inclined his head in
her direction. "It wasn't just a part. She planned,
set up, and executed every detail of my release
with no help from any government or private
agency."

A rush of murmurs swept the audience.

"She did so at the risk of her life and danger
of her own captivity." His lips thinned. "And
believe me, the latter is no small risk, as she
knew very well. Let me tell you a few things
about Ronnie Dalton. You all know her work.
Among other stories she did Jed Corbin's camera
work in San Salvador, the Los Angeles riots, and
the hurricane coverage at Homestead.

"What you haven't heard about is a few other
episodes in her life. That she turned in film of
atrocities in Kuwait to the Human Rights Commission rather than sending it to the networks."

Ronnie could feel the heat in her cheeks.
She should never have told Gabe about that, she
thought in disgust. He was making her sound
noble, for heaven's sake.

"You probably also never heard that in

Somalia she drove an unescorted relief truck to a village in an area beset by bandits."

Her mouth fell open.

He smiled at her. "Sorry, Ronnie, I know you're going to want revenge after this." He turned back to the reporters. "And you might be interested in the fact that she paid for that relief truck out of her own pocket and offered similar help to the homeless in Homestead. There are probably several other instances you can dig up that will prove what kind of woman she is. I've never met a braver or more honest individual or one more worthy of representing the United States around the world." He paused and then added soberly, "There are a few things that aren't as wonderful in her life, and she won't talk about those either. To save you from digging them up, you'll find a complete dossier on Ronnie Dalton with the material Dan will hand out. What won't be in the dossier is that I will have the extreme honor of marrying this remarkable woman tomorrow afternoon at four o'clock." He held up his hand to stop the outbreak of questions. "I've been away a long time and I'm homesick as hell. It's my hope that the American people will be generous enough to permit my wife to come home with me." He paused. "Because I won't come home without her."

Ronnie stared at him, stunned.

"You can see she's a little surprised. We agreed to go public, but she didn't expect me to put her on the spot like this." He grimaced. "She'll make me suffer for it later."

He ignored the laughter as he reached out his hand to pull her to her feet. "Come on, Ronnie, I'll let them ask you three questions and then we'll escape from here."

Her knees were shaking and she needed his support as she joined him in front of the microphones. "Don't you dare leave me," she said in an undertone.

"I'll be here." He held her hand as they faced the cameras. "Be kind to her. She deserves it." He lifted Ronnie's hand to his lips and kissed it.

The old-world gesture should have looked phony coming from such a contemporary powerhouse as Gabe Falkner. It didn't appear anything but graceful and caring and just right. *He* was just right. She couldn't stand here and stare at him. Cripes, she must look a complete dunce.

She straightened her shoulders and turned to face the audience. "Okay, I'm here. I don't want to be here. I'd much rather be out there with you. So fire away and let me blow this joint."

The room erupted and Gabe stepped forward. "Three questions."

"How did you manage to secure Falkner's release when the other attempts were unsuccessful?"

"I had the help of my father."

"You'll find several references to Ronnie's father in the dossier." Gabe pointed to another reporter. "Next."

"We've never heard of you in connection with Falkner. How long has this relationship been going on?"

"Years."

She pointed to James Ketrick. "You, Jim."

Ketrick was smiling cynically. "You're trying to tell us you rescued Gabe Falkner because you love him, Ronnie?"

Cripes, there were going to be soppy headlines from New York to Bangkok. She looked at Gabe in panic. He was smiling ruefully at her, giving her support, strength, and warmth, making everything all right again.

Shock rippled through her and she inhaled sharply.

"Ronnie," Gabe prompted softly.

She tore her gaze away and faced the reporters. "Yes," she said shakily. "What else could I do? I love him."

She stepped back and Gabe's arm immediately went around her. "That's all." He nodded to Dan, who immediately began distributing the news releases. The distraction allowed them to reach the door without interference, and the guards had been given orders to let no one leave the room for five minutes after they had made their getaway.

"You did very well," he said as he swept her down the hall toward her suite. "Just the right amount of professionalism and sentiment. For a minute I thought that honesty of yours was going to get us into trouble."

"Soppy." She didn't look at him. "They'd be nuts to believe us."

"You were very credible."

Credible. She almost laughed hysterically. She had felt stripped, naked. "You should have told me you were going to lay everything out on the table."

"I wanted to go public with the whole package. If we're perfectly open at the outset, there won't be any scandal stories dribbling in over the next few weeks to undermine us." He added, "Besides, you were nervous enough as it was. Now it's over."

"It's just begun. Now there's no place to hide."

"You won't need a place to hide."

"And you shouldn't have told them you wouldn't go home without me. You're going to look like an ass when you have to do it."

"I decided to up the ante. If they want to get the captive home, they have to take you too."

"Look, even if Immigration goes along with us, it will take a long time."

"Then we'll wait."

Commitment. She should have known he would go all the way once he had decided to help her. She walked faster. "And what's this about the marriage ceremony?"

"Strike while the iron is hot. Today they write about a heroine who fulfills their imaginations."

"Who is incidentally a criminal," she added grimly.

He ignored the qualification. "And tomorrow we give them pictures of the bride to stir their hearts." Gabe stopped before the door of her suite. "You'll need a wedding gown. What size? Eight?"

"Six. Where are you going to get a wedding gown?"

"Dan will find something appropriate. It may not be haute couture, but no one will expect that on such short notice."

It was going too fast for her. Wedding gowns and revelations she had kept secret all her life. "Are you sure you want to do this?"

"I'm sure." He stopped before her door. "I've never been more sure of anything. It's going to be fine, Ronnie."

She was not nearly as confident. She had thought she was going to be the only one to pay if this gamble didn't succeed, but Gabe was making vows, involving himself too deeply. "You could back out now. It would be okay with me."

He brushed a kiss on the tip of her nose. "It wouldn't be okay with me. I'll join you in your suite for dinner at seven if that's all right."

"Sounds fine."

She watched him as he turned and walked away from her. It was the first time he had kissed her, and it was a caress he could have given to a sister or a maiden aunt . . . or Orphan Annie.

He looked over his shoulder and saw her still standing there. "Okay?"

She smiled with effort. "Sure."

She quickly entered the room and shut the door.

It wasn't okay. Until that moment when she had been forced to answer Jim's question, she had deliberately blocked the truth from her mind.

Now she knew. And Lord help her, she did love Gabe Falkner.

Dan arrived at her suite later that afternoon carrying a large glossy-white cardboard box and several smaller ones of various sizes piled on top of it.

"Good heavens, you look like the delivery boy for one of those 1930s movies," Ronnie said as she stepped aside to let him inside.

"You mean the ones where Ginger Rogers goes shopping while Fred Astaire is busy dancing on the ceiling?" He grinned. "I would have had them delivered, but I wanted to make sure you got them. Gabe wouldn't be pleased if anything went wrong."

"Gabe said he'd buy a dress, not an entire wardrobe."

"I admit I got a little carried away." Dan dumped the boxes on the bed. "But the woman at the department store said you'll need all of it." He waved a hand. "You know, stockings and garters and slips and shoes . . ." He frowned.

"I wasn't sure about the shoes. I had to guess. Seven?"

"Pretty good. Six and a half, but I can stuff the toes with cotton."

He gave a huge sigh of relief. "Then I won't have to go back. I felt like a bull in a china shop surrounded by all those veils and gowns and whatnots."

"Gabe shouldn't have imposed on you. I could have taken care of it myself. I've been going crazy with nothing to do."

"Gabe was afraid you'd be followed by reporters. He thought you'd had enough of being the center of attention for a time."

"For *all* time," she said fervently. "Do you often do these little odd jobs for Gabe?"

"Everything from making appointments with the president to arranging an intimate weekend with Mora Renord. I do it all." He immediately looked a little uneasy. "I guess I shouldn't have mentioned Mora."

She tried to hide the sharp twinge she had received at the thought of Gabe's former mistress. "Why not? You must know why Gabe is marrying me. It's all a farce."

"Is it?" His gaze searched her face. "Gabe's behaving very strangely about all this."

She looked down at the boxes on the bed. "I wouldn't know. I haven't known him long enough to judge."

"Well, I have and it's not like Gabe to . . ." He shrugged. "But it's not my business. He wouldn't thank me for analyzing his moves."

She lifted her chin. "I suppose you don't approve of Gabe marrying me."

"I didn't say that," he said. "Look, it was my job to set up the exchange of Gabe for those two journalists. How do you think I felt all these months when I could have heard any day that Gabe had been executed? You got him out. You deserve any payback we can give you. Heck, if marriage will help you get what you want, I'll marry you myself."

His earnestness caught her off guard. "Good grief, the suitors are standing in line," she said awkwardly, then hurriedly changed the subject. "How long have you known Gabe?"

"Over ten years. We were reporters together in Beirut, and when Gabe went on to greater things, I went with him. I couldn't have found better coattails to ride on."

"I don't think you like free rides. Gabe said you were a good man to have around in tight corners."

"We've been in a few." He smiled. "And so have you. That mess in Said Ababa must have been a little dicey."

"You could say that." She asked with a pretense of casualness, "If you've been together that long, then you must know his family."

"His parents are dead. He has only one sister, Carrie, and her daughter, Daisy."

"What is she like?"

"Like Gabe. Brilliant, absolutely self-sufficient. She married an oilman from Houston and promptly took over the company. She's vice-president and practically runs both the firm and the social scene in Houston."

"Are she and Gabe close?"

"Fairly. But they don't see much of each other."

"Because she's too busy running Houston and he's too busy running the rest of the world," Ronnie guessed.

"Probably. Gabe's a born leader. He gets a kick out of holding the reins."

"And leaders who do their job right have no time to devote to a family." He was only confirming what she had surmised about Gabe.

Dan frowned. "It's not as if he isn't always there when he's needed."

"I'm sure he is." She had known that about him too. She knew many things about Gabe, and yet there were gaps she had never been able to fill in over the years.

Dan turned and moved toward the door. "I'd better hustle. I've got to fly the helicopter over to the airport and pick up John Grant and bring him to the palace."

"You're flying yourself? I thought David Carroll was the pilot."

"Dave does most of the general business flying, but I usually pilot Gabe. I only brought Dave when we did the pickup in Said Ababa in case there was trouble. I wasn't sure what we'd find when we got there." He smiled. "But you had the situation well in hand."

"And got a knockout punch as a reward."

He looked pained. "Let's drop the subject. I don't think Gabe would appreciate me keeping the topic fresh in your mind." He opened the door. "If there's any problem with those wedding duds, let me know."

"Wait," she said impulsively, starting after him. "Could I go with you?"

He hesitated. "Gabe doesn't want you to be wandering around in public."

"I won't be wandering around. I'll even stay

in the helicopter, if you like. I'll go crazy cooped up in here for the rest of the afternoon."

He shrugged. "You're welcome to come, if you're sure you want to go. It will be a pretty boring trip."

She had a hunger to learn about all the details and people that made up Gabe's world. Going along would give her an opportunity to get to know these two men who were Gabe's good friends and to listen to them talk about Gabe. She could even ask casual questions that would reveal layers and depths she had not yet been able to probe. "I won't be bored."

When Gabe arrived at the suite that night, he was wearing jeans and a navy shirt that made his eyes appear bluer than usual. Somehow she had expected him to seem different now that she knew she loved him, but he was the same— tough, mature, completely male.

He raised his brows. "May I come in?"

"Oh, sure." She backed away from the door. "The servant already brought dinner." She gestured to the roll-away table across the room. "Sit down."

"For a minute I wasn't certain if you were

going to throw me out or not." He seated himself opposite her and shook out his napkin. "You looked at me as if you weren't sure if I'd had my rabies shots."

"That's for dogs." She picked up her fork and attacked her salad.

"There is a correlation. When I left you this afternoon, I wasn't sure if I was in the doghouse or not. There was a possibility the shock about the news conference had worn off and you were mad as hell."

"You'd know if I was mad. I'm pretty transparent." Not too transparent, she hoped. She was scared even to look at him. "I'm not sure you should have mentioned Evan in that dossier. He should be safe, but you focused a lot of attention on him this afternoon."

His expression hardened. "Stop worrying about him. He didn't worry about you." He changed the subject. "Dan told me he brought you the wedding gown this afternoon."

She nodded. "Do you want to see it?"

"Not before tomorrow. It's bad luck." He took a roll from the covered basket on the table. "Or don't you believe in traditions?"

She watched in fascination as he broke the roll in two. His hands were strong and broad

and capable. Even in that blackness at Mekhit
she had sensed their strength.

Light in the darkness.

"Ronnie?"

She looked away from his hands. "Oh, I never
thought much about them. Do you?"

He nodded. "I think they hold us together
and give us stability. We all move too fast these
days. We'd spin away into the stratosphere without something to hold on to."

She would hold on forever.

"I guess you're right." She smiled at him.
"Eat your steak. Protein."

"Yes, ma'am."

Lord, she loved his smile, that dry intonation
in his voice, the way he lifted his brows. Love was
brimming, overflowing, and she quickly lowered
her gaze to her own plate and began to eat.

"I hear you went to the airport with Dan to
fetch John."

She nodded. "He's a nice guy."

"He likes you too. Dan said he's never heard
John talk so much all the time he's known him."

She had used all her journalistic skills to make
sure John Grant talked extensively and exclusive-
ly on one subject: Gabe. "He's very interesting."

She tried to keep up her end of the conversation during the meal, but it was difficult when she only wanted to look at him, savor the characteristics that made him Gabe Falkner. Because she was staring at him so hungrily, she noticed something that made her frown.

"Why are you looking at me like that?" Gabe asked. "Do I have a smudge on my face?"

"Two. Right beneath your eyes. You didn't sleep again," Ronnie said. "This can't go on. Why don't you go to the doctor and get some pills?"

"Because I don't want to." He reached for the carafe. "More coffee?"

"No, and you don't either. You don't need anything else to keep you awake," she said. "It's my fault, isn't it?"

"I told you, it's aftershock. You have nothing to do with it."

"It *is* my fault. You've done nothing but plan and telephone and set up press conferences since the moment we arrived here. You should have gone away to rest."

"I will later. There's plenty of time after we get you settled properly."

She had doubts if she would ever be settled to her satisfaction, but there was no use arguing with him on that subject. "It's not going to happen overnight and you'll be a wreck if this keeps on."

"Ronnie, it's not your fault I can't sleep."

"But maybe I can help." She stood up and strode toward the gauze-draped bed across the room. "Come on. I used to do this with Jed to help him relax." She glanced over her shoulder and saw him still sitting where she had left him. "Well, come on."

"I won't accept sex as physical therapy, no matter what Jed Corbin did," he said grimly.

"Oh, for goodness sake, Jed was my friend. He would have laughed at the idea of jumping me." She stood by the bed. "I learned massage from a woman in a bath house in Istanbul and I'm pretty good at it. I used to massage his shoulders to take out the kinks. Take off your shirt."

He stood looking at her a moment and then stood up and began to unbutton his shirt. "Poor Corbin."

"Because he was my friend?"

He stripped off his shirt and threw it on the chair. "Because I'd bet he wouldn't have laughed at the idea of jumping you." He came toward her. "He probably went through the tortures of the damned when you put your hands all over him."

He stopped before her. His massive shoulders

gleamed in the lamplight, and she realized she wanted to reach out and touch the springy dark hair on his chest, to step closer and rub against him. The air was suddenly charged and hard to breathe.

"Not all over him," she whispered. "Just his back and shoulders."

"That can be enough. Muscles and nerves are all connected," he said thickly. "And want to be connected even more . . . intimately."

She was starting to tremble. "Don't you want me to help you?"

"I want you to touch me." He tore his gaze away from her and lay down on the bed and rolled over on his stomach. "Do it."

She took a deep breath and sat down beside him. She hesitated a moment and then gently put her hands on his back. She could feel the muscles tense as if a whip had touched them. She knew how he felt. A sensual shock ran through her that was as hot as it was electrifying. "Relax." The words were for herself as much as for him. She began rubbing, her thumbs digging, trying to loosen the tautness. His skin felt smooth and warm, his muscles sinewy and sleek. She tried to think of something to say that would lessen the tension pervading the room. "And you're wrong, it was never like that with Jed."

"Then he was a fool." The words were muffled by the pillow.

Her hands worked upward to his shoulders. "Not everyone has the good taste to appreciate my type. He's mad about his wife, Ysabel." Cripes, her palms were beginning to tingle with every movement, the heat shooting up her wrists. "They live on an island off the Pacific coast. I was there once." She tried to keep her voice steady. "It's lovely."

"Is it?"

"Yes. Where do you live now?" Her fingers kneaded the nape of his neck and she felt the brush of thick short hairs against the top of her hands. Her breasts were swelling, acutely sensitive as they pushed against the cloth of her bra.

"Dallas, principally. I have a home in Aspen too."

"Aspen, that's very posh."

"Not my place. The cabin is pretty basic. I only go up there in the winter when it snows. I like the cold after the hot summers in Texas."

Cold. The concept of anything but heat was completely alien to her at this moment.

"Someday I'd like to live in Iowa," she said. "I remember reading about the county fairs and the fields of corn and wheat."

"The all-American girl."

"Did you see that BBC broadcast tonight? They're calling me the Star-Spangled Bride. It's enough to make you vomit."

"It's a good sound bite."

"Corny."

"As Iowa and county fairs." A long shudder racked his body. "You'd better stop this."

She didn't want to stop. She wanted to keep on touching him. She wanted him to touch her. "Why?"

"It's not relaxing me. It's making me worse."

She looked at the muscles of his back, now more contracted than ever. She had done this to him with her touch. The realization caused the muscles of her stomach to clench. "You do seem . . . harder."

"Much harder." He sat up and swung his feet to the floor. He didn't look at her as he got jerkily to his feet. "The Red December has nothing on you as far as torture goes."

She could feel the heat in her cheeks. Her breasts were lifting and falling with every rapid breath. "Then why didn't you stop me?"

He moved toward the door, snatching his shirt from the chair as he passed. "It seemed worth it at the time. I believe I've turned into a masochist."

"Gabe."

He turned and looked at her, and when he saw her expression, he shook his head. "When we make love, it won't be because you want to heal me. I want a hell of a lot more than that."

Frustration and guilt surged through her as she watched the door close behind him. It may have started because she wanted to help him, but she had continued because she had not been able to resist the temptation of touching him, making him feel the whirlpool of emotion that was pulling her toward him. She had wanted sex, but she had wanted something else, something more. She had wanted to belong to him. She *needed* to belong to him.

It could still happen. It was clear he did want her and they were being married tomorrow. Heck, she had a chance to clear up the misunderstandings and win the grand prize. She might not be able to keep it for long but . . .

She quickly shied away from that train of thought. She wouldn't think beyond the wedding tomorrow.

Wedding gowns, flowers, guests, and a holy man saying words over them. The concept was as foreign to her as she could ever have imagined. It was the kind of thing that happened to those nice, wholesome women who lived in Iowa and put up preserves for county fairs, not to her.

Yet it was happening and she could feel the excitement beginning to build at the thought of tomorrow.

SIX

"You look wonderful," Gabe said.

"It's the gown that's wonderful." She gently touched the skirt of the exquisite gown, a simple drift of ivory silk that framed her bare shoulders with fine Valenciennes lace.

"It's not the gown."

"Are you sure it's okay?" She gestured to the white rose headdress that held her veil in place. "It makes me look more like an old-time Gibson girl than ever."

"There's nothing wrong with Gibson girls." He stepped forward, reached into his jacket, and brought out a small jeweler's box. "I have something for you."

"What is it? The ring?"

"No, Dan has the ring. I chose a simple band. This is a bride's gift. It's a tradition."

"I know you said you believed in tradition, but this isn't a traditional wedding." She opened the box. Earrings. Exquisite pearl drops cascading from small studs channel-set with sapphires and rubies. "Red, white, and blue," she murmured huskily.

"Every wedding should have something blue, and I thought the theme was fitting for a Star-Spangled Bride. I'll give you the matching necklace when you become a citizen."

"I wish I was as confident as you. Thank you." She moved to the mirror and started to put them on. "They're lovely." Her voice was tremulous. "I'm sure they'll photograph beautifully."

He stood behind her, so close she could feel the heat from his body. The scent of his spicy after-shave drifted to her. "I'm sure they will too."

She met his gaze in the mirror. He was staring at her with an intentness that made her breathless. "I suppose we should leave."

"Yes." He didn't move.

She reached up and pulled down the veil to cover her face. "Another veil," she said shakily. "A man probably thought this one up too."

"I don't agree," he said. "At this point in a relationship, a man has no use for barriers."

She was glad of the veil. She felt naked, helpless, completely vulnerable, and more womanly than she had ever felt in her life. She searched desperately for something to say that would permit her to regain her equilibrium. "At least it hides the bruise."

His expression changed, became shuttered. "Yes, that's one use for it." He took a step back. "We'd better get going. Our friends in the press will be getting restless."

"More questions?"

He shook his head. "I told them pictures would be permitted, but if anyone tried for an impromptu interview with you, he'd be thrown out."

"They'll try anyway."

"Dan will run interference." He took her hand and led her toward the door. "Don't worry, we'll take care of everything."

Again she felt that overwhelming sense of womanliness. It was strange to yield, to be protected and treasured. Such treatment in large doses would probably annoy her to madness, but for once it felt infinitely precious.

Her hand tightened on his as he led her out of the suite.

• • •

The ceremony took place in the beautiful little chapel on the grounds of the palace and was like a strange poignant dream for Ronnie. She was only vaguely aware of banks of flowers— purple hyacinths, scarlet poinsettias, and white roses—the dark-skinned clergyman in his sober black attire and crisp white collar, Gabe standing next to her, straight and strong. She wondered sadly how she would have felt at this moment if she knew Gabe was marrying her because he loved her.

"Ronnie?" Gabe was frowning with concern, his gaze fixed intently on her face. He reached out and took her hand.

She cast a quick glance at the clergyman before she whispered, "It's not time for you to take my hand yet."

"Ask me if I care," he said gruffly. His hand tightened in possession and affection as it had when he had led her from the suite.

He had sensed her sadness and had acted to dispel it with his usual forcefulness. He *did* care about her. He might not love her, but he did care. She smiled tremulously as she nodded at Gabe and then looked back at the clergyman.

A few minutes later the ceremony was over,
and the kiss he gave her was so tender, it might
even have been called loving.

Then he was turning, leading her down the
ribbon-lined aisle and out of the chapel across
the rose garden to the reception in the palace.

The rest of the afternoon passed in a blur
of impressions. The long white damask-covered
table with its array of fine foods, the ice swan
rising in crystal beauty in the middle of the
table. Her meeting with His Majesty, Sheikh
Ben Raschid, and his lovely red-haired wife,
Sabrina. Either Gabe or Dan was always at her
elbow and she only had to smile, nod, and drink
champagne.

"A lovely wedding, Mrs. Falkner."

Mrs. Falkner. The words had been said so
many times in the last hour that she had almost
become accustomed to them. She turned and
smiled automatically at the short balding man in
a blue suit who had uttered them. She didn't
recognized him. "You're very kind."

Dan glanced at Gabe, who was across the
room, and then took a protective step nearer
Ronnie. "Good of you to come, Pilsner."

"I wouldn't have missed it."

"Ronnie, this is Herb Pilsner," Dan said. "He's
a very big man in Immigration."

Ronnie stiffened as she looked into Pilsner's cool green eyes. "How do you do."

"Actually, not too well." His lips thinned. "I'm tired and jet-lagged and a little annoyed. I was rousted out of bed in the middle of the night by Senator Koras and told to expedite your paperwork so that Falkner could bring you back into the country with him."

"Why don't we go out on the terrace?" Dan quickly ushered them out the French doors.

"That isn't necessary, Bredlowe," Pilsner said. "I don't have much more to say and I'll be making a statement to the press anyway." He turned to Ronnie. "I don't give a damn about Koras and his friends on Capitol Hill or this media blitz Falkner has instigated to get you citizenship. This wedding is as phony as a three-dollar bill and I don't like phonies. To me you're no better than a Haitian boat person or an Italian factory worker. It's my job to see that the laws regarding immigration are obeyed, to protect the citizens of the United States, and there's no reason why I should give you preferential treatment. It's not right and it's not fair."

Ronnie felt as if she'd been punched in the stomach. She hadn't realized how high she had permitted her hopes to rise until Pilsner had crushed them.

"There are extenuating circumstances," Dan said. "I don't think you can judge—"

"Don't argue with him, Dan," Ronnie interrupted quietly. "You're not going to change his mind. Besides, can't you see the man is right?" Her gaze met Pilsner's. "I respect your position. I didn't think there was any chance, but Gabe—" She had to stop to steady her voice. "Gabe doesn't give up easily."

For an instant Pilsner's expression softened. "It was the charge in El Salvador. I can't overlook that, Mrs. Falkner. It would be totally irresponsible of me." His expression hardened. "And the fact that you've been traveling unlawfully for years on a forged passport. That can't be tolerated. It sets a bad example and extradition proceedings may have to be—"

"The hell they will." Gabe stood in the doorway and slammed the French doors shut behind him. "You can't take her as long as she stays in Sedikhan. Sedikhan is an absolute monarchy and has no extradition treaty with the U.S."

"Quite true," Pilsner said. "But the minute she steps across the border, the situation changes." His glance shifted to Ronnie. "Your chosen profession demands a good deal of travel and you're not going to be satisfied staying here. When you make that mistake, we'll have you."

"For God's sake, she's not a criminal," Gabe said violently.

"She is to the U.S. government," Pilsner said. He inclined his head to Ronnie. "Good day, Mrs. Falkner. I regret not being able to help you." He moved toward the French doors. "As I said, it was a lovely wedding."

"Bastard," Gabe muttered as the doors closed behind Pilsner.

"What do we do?" Dan asked uneasily. "He's going to make a statement to the press."

"Go deal with them," Gabe said. "Paint Ronnie as a helpless victim of bureaucracy. Spread it on thick." He took Ronnie's elbow and propelled her across the terrace toward the steps leading to the garden. "Tell them we'll issue another statement after we return from our honeymoon."

"Where are you going?" Dan asked.

"Tanadahl. It's isolated enough to keep everyone off our backs until we can regroup."

Dan nodded and disappeared back into the palace.

"Where's Tanadahl?" Ronnie asked dully.

"It's a house I own in the desert. I stay there when I spend long periods here in Sedikhan." He glanced at her. "Are you okay? You look a little pale."

"I'm all right." She shrugged. "I knew it was too good to be true. You're the one who was sure you could pull off a happy ending." She looked straight ahead. "Do I have time to change out of this gown before we go to this hideout of yours?"

"No, you'd get waylaid. We're going straight to the helicopter. I'll have Dan bring some clothes for you tomorrow night and your camera is already in the helicopter. That's all that's important, isn't it?"

"Yes, that's all that's important." It had been true before this all started. She doubted if it would ever be true again. She tossed the bouquet she was still carrying onto a marble bench they were passing and brusquely picked up her skirts as they approached the helicopter. "I can do without anything else if I have my camera."

Tanadahl was not a palace, not even a very large house, but a charming residence of white stucco and red tile that looked as though it could have been transported from Mexico or southern California. From the air its lovely landscaped terrace and garden looked less impressive than comfortable. The place radiated an atmosphere of . . . Ronnie mentally searched for the right word. Intimacy.

"Well?" Gabe asked as he waved at Dave and the pilot lifted the helicopter off the ground and headed back toward Marasef.

"I like it," Ronnie said. "It's much better than the palace. I'm not into all that grandeur."

"Neither am I." He led her across the courtyard to the front door. "That's why I bought this place. Sedikhan is a very enlightened and progressive country, and whenever I have to be anywhere in this part of the world, I stay here."

She took off the veil and headpiece she still wore. "I need a bath." She looked at him. "And then we need to talk."

He nodded. "Pilsner threw a rod in the works. We have to find a way to get around it."

He was not giving up, she realized in despair. He would not admit it was hopeless. He would never give up.

He took her elbow and escorted her into the oak-tiled foyer that opened into a huge sunken living room. The interior of the house appeared to be as charming as the exterior, featuring high ceilings, book-lined walls, and a stone fireplace. Pearl-gray cushioned couches and chairs repeated the color of the lush carpet and offered a striking contrast to the deep burgundy of the miniblinds shading the long windows on the south wall and the occasional pillows tossed on the couch. Though the decor was of no particular period, the emphasis was clearly on comfort and offered only a few touches of Mediterranean opulence in the mother-of-pearl inlaid screen and a wonderfully crafted gold camel on the coffee table.

"We're on our own here," Gabe said. "There are no permanent servants. A crew comes from a nearby village twice a week to clean and garden. We shouldn't starve. I never know when I'll have to make a trip over here, so I give orders that the kitchen be always stocked."

"That's good."

"Your bedroom is second on the right." He gestured down the hall to the left of the foyer. "Take your time. Relax. I'll come and get you in an hour or so and we'll see what we can round up in the way of food. If you need anything, call me."

"I will." She turned and walked toward the bedroom he had indicated.

"Ronnie."

She turned to look at him.

He frowned, troubled. "It's going to be fine. I know you're upset by this Pilsner mess, but this is only a setback."

She smiled wearily and nodded. "See you."

He didn't understand. He had been an American all his life and couldn't comprehend what it was like to want something so much that it was an ache inside you, to want to *belong*. He wanted to help her, intended to sacrifice and work, do everything he could to make her dream come true, but even he didn't realize how deep this disappointment went.

Good heavens, why was she feeling so sorry for herself? she thought in self-disgust. It was her own fault for allowing her hopes to be raised when she knew the odds. She would just have to adjust to this dilemma and make sure her defeat didn't hurt Gabe.

But she didn't have to worry about that right now.

She was here with Gabe and she would do what she had done all her life to survive and make life worth living.

She would seize the moment she had been given.

• • •

She hesitated for a moment outside Gabe's door. Good grief, she felt foolish. He would probably hoot with laughter when he saw her. Well, she couldn't stay here all night. Seize the moment, dammit. She threw open the door and stepped into the room. After all her mental preparations she was immediately deflated by the sound of the shower running in the adjoining bathroom. Not yet. She drew a deep breath and silently shut the door. She should welcome the postponement, not be disappointed. It gave her a few more minutes to prepare herself.

The shower was turned off and she could hear movement. He would be here in a moment.

The bathroom door opened and she braced herself.

He was naked; his tousled dark hair had been hastily dried, but it still gleamed with moisture.

She swallowed. "Hello."

He stopped in the doorway, stiffening as he saw her standing there draped in nothing but the wedding veil she was using as a shawl. "What the hell are you doing here?"

"At the moment I'm shivering. I didn't have

anything else to wear and I knew you liked veils, so I—"

He cut her off. "I suppose you have a reason for this."

She tried to shrug carelessly. "I thought I was making it pretty clear."

"Not to me. I told you I didn't need sex to relax me."

It hadn't occurred to her that he would assume she was here for that purpose. The scene in her suite last night seemed a thousand years ago. "That's not why I came."

"Go on," he said curtly.

She hadn't expected him to be this wary or herself to be this uncertain. She searched wildly for an answer that would make her feel less vulnerable. She tried to make her tone flippant. "It's been a bad day. I need to take the edge off."

"Then get the hell out of here," he said harshly.

She gazed at him helplessly. "I can't," she whispered. "I have to have you."

His gaze narrowed on her face. "Me or anyone?"

"You." She moved to stand before him and slowly let the veil fall open to reveal her breasts.

Her voice was uneven. "I lied. It has to be you, Gabe."

"You're damn right it does."

He picked her up and carried her to the bed.

She could feel the warmth of his skin through the thin veiling, the strength of his arms as he placed her on the bed and followed her down.

The veil was ripped away and thrown . . . somewhere.

He stared down at her, his breath coming harshly. "Damn, you're . . ." His hand reached out and closed around her breast. It instantly responded; her entire body was responding. Heat seemed to travel from his grasp to every part of her. "Lovely . . ." He watched the flush come to her cheeks, her nipples grow taut. "This is lovely."

His head slowly lowered and his mouth touched one hard nipple. Her chest was lifting and falling as his tongue followed, caressed and teased. Then his whole mouth enveloped her and he began sucking strongly as his other hand kneaded and plumped her other breast.

She bit her lip to keep from screaming at the incredible sensation.

He was making sounds himself, deep, groaning sounds of need that were as exciting as his mouth on her breast. He was over her, straddling her. He began rubbing against her, flesh on flesh, hair on hair, in a frantic sexual rhythm.

He lifted his head. "I can't—it's been too long." A shudder went through Gabe. "I'm sorry. It's got to be quick."

"That's all right." Her arms clutched him tightly. "It doesn't matter." Nothing mattered but that she was close to him, closer than she had ever been before, and would soon be even closer.

He drew a deep breath and said, "No, it's not fair. I'll try to . . ." He parted her thighs and began rubbing, petting her, tugging at the tight curls. "I wanted to spend more time here. . . ." Two fingers moved down and entered.

She arched upward with a little cry.

"Tight," he murmured. "So tight." He began to stroke in and out slowly as he reached up with his other hand and searched for the nub. When he found it, she cried out again.

He began to rotate the nub while he stroked her, gradually increasing both tempos until she received a sensual jolt with every movement.

She could hear the animallike cries coming from her throat, but they seemed to have no connection with her. The only awareness she had was of that part of her his fingers were caressing, stimulating.

"You like it?" he asked fiercely. Another finger joined the others within her. "More?"

"More." Her head was thrashing back and forth on the pillow. "Gabe, it's—"

"Shh . . ." His hands were gone and he was nudging against her. "I have to be careful. You're so narrow."

She was agonizingly empty and he was too slow. Her hands grabbed his hips and tugged him forward. "To hell with careful," she said. "More."

He sat up, looking down at her. "Ronnie, I don't want to let go." He laughed desperately. "That's a lie, but I'm afraid—"

"*More.*"

He plunged forward to the hilt.

Pain and then an exquisite fullness, a joining.

"Lord!" He went still, deep within her.

Fullness but still a hunger.

"Don't pay any attention," she gasped as her fingers dug into his hips. "It doesn't hurt. Get on with it."

"It's a difficult thing to ignore." An expression of desire so intense it was almost pain crossed his face. "Lord . . . it feels good."

He liked the tightness, she realized hazily. She instinctively tried to give him more.

A shudder went through him. "Don't do that yet. I'm too—" He looked down at her and his hands reached out to tangle in her hair. "Lord, you're completely . . . beautiful."

He meant it. She was beautiful to him at this moment. She knew she would look back on this moment with tenderness, but it wasn't tenderness she wanted now. "For heaven's sake, don't pay me compliments. This isn't the time."

His laughter again had an element of desperation in it. "I'm trying to keep from acting like a sex maniac and hurting you."

She said, "I want you. I want this. Don't make me ask again." She tried to smile jauntily. "Or I might just get up and walk away."

"The hell you will." He started moving, thrusting slow, fast, long, short.

His hands moved under her, lifting her to every thrust.

The tempo was feverish, primitive, almost animalistic. Gabe's lips were drawn back from his teeth, his cheeks hollowed with strain.

Ronnie could hear herself pleading mindlessly as she met thrust with thrust.

When the climax came, it was like being torn

from darkness into brilliant sunlight. She was scarcely conscious of Gabe's low cry as he gained his own satisfaction and collapsed on top of her.

Pleasure. Madness. Closeness. Bonding.

Forever.

SEVEN

"Well, that was a surprise." Gabe drew her into the hollow of his shoulder. "In more ways than one. Would you care to tell me how it happens you were still a virgin?"

"You didn't seem to mind at the time." She raised herself on one elbow to frown at him. "Or did you? Were you pretending?"

"I assure you it's impossible to pretend under those circumstances."

Her frown cleared. "I thought so, but I had to be sure. I'll be better next time. I promise."

"Don't. I don't think I could stand it." He pulled her down again. "You were quite enough as it was. I was just curious. You've led a pretty rough life. It would have been natural for you to take comfort where you could."

"I could never see what all the shouting was

all about." She suddenly giggled. "Until I started shouting myself. I wasn't very dignified, was I?"

"No. You didn't shout; it was more like a seductive moan, but dignified isn't how I'd describe you," he said thickly. "Passionate, beautiful, moving."

"Well, I did plenty of moving."

"Stop being flip. I'm trying to tell you something."

"What?"

"This." He lowered his head and kissed her on the lips.

Sweetness. Dawn after the storm.

She closed her eyes. "Oh, I like that."

"Then open your eyes and look at me."

Her lids slowly opened and she dreamily looked up at him. "You've got wonderful cheekbones. They photograph like gangbusters."

"I'm glad I have one feature you like." His eyes twinkled. "No, two."

"Definitely two." Sweet heavens, she loved him so *much*. She suddenly hurled herself into his arms and held him tight. "It was good, wasn't it? It was good and real and—"

"Shh, it was all of those things." He gently stroked her back. "Why are you so panicky?"

"I want it to go on. I want it to last." She

added quickly, "Forget I said that. I didn't mean it. It's the stupid kind of thing a woman who had just had her first man would say. You mustn't feel any pressure. I don't really—"

He stopped her with his lips. "I've felt pressure since the moment you walked into my life. Why do you think I didn't drag you into bed last night? Because I've never felt like this before. I feel as responsible as hell. I want to guard you and take care of you and be everything to you that you want me to be." He kissed her gently on the nose. "Even Daddy Warbucks."

"I never meant to make you feel like that," she whispered.

"It goes with the territory when you love someone."

She looked at him in shock that was comprised of as much fear as joy.

"It surprised me too," he said ruefully. "I liked my life the way it was. No strings and the only responsibility strictly on the professional level. Then you appeared on the scene and suddenly everything changed."

"Yes, it did." Her voice was muffled.

He feathered a kiss on her temple. "I'd appreciate a similar declaration."

So he could feel even more pressure and more

responsible for her. So that he would be bound to her no matter how much it cost him. Dammit, she should never have lost control and triggered this confession on his part. No, she was glad she had done it, she thought fiercely. It might be selfish, but it couldn't hurt anyone for her to know he loved her. She could fix the rest.

She buried her head deeper in his shoulder. "I can't tell you something that's not true. I don't love you."

He went still. "The hell you don't."

"I don't," she insisted.

He lifted her chin with his fingers and stared down at her. "You're lying to me."

"I'm not lying." She forced herself to sit up and look directly into his eyes. "I like you. And I love this, but if that's not enough for you, I'll have to leave."

"What are you afraid of?"

"Nothing. I'm not afraid of anything." She reached for the veil, which had landed at the foot of the bed. "And maybe it would be better if I did go."

"The hell you will." He roughly pulled her back into his arms. "You'll stay with me."

Relief surged through her. She had been afraid he would let her go and she didn't think she could

surrender him without giving herself a little time.
"Not if you expect me to swear undying love
for you."

"Dammit, you do—" He stopped, then said,
"I don't know what's going on with that con-
voluted thinking process of yours, but I won't
argue with you right now." His voice hardened
with determination. "Just know this, Ronnie. I'm
not going to let you go."

"I don't want to go." She paused. "Not yet."

He shook his head. "Never." He rolled her
over on her back and parted her thighs. "This
is it, Ronnie, the real McCoy. Get used to the
idea."

"This is wonderful," Ronnie said when she
could talk without gasping. "Like a roller-coaster
ride, but the ending is better. I've always thought
that gliding slowly back into the starting ramp
sort of took something away. They should find
a way to catch the cars in the chute like they do
jet planes on aircraft carriers."

"Well, which am I?" Gabe lazily circled the
areola of her nipple with an index finger. "A
roller coaster or a jet plane?"

"Neither." She kissed him lovingly on the
mouth. "You're the bee's knees."

"Sounds minuscule. I believe I'm insulted."

"Don't be. You're just right. Delicious." She sat bolt upright in bed. "Which reminds me. I'm starving. How do you expect me to absorb all these new skills if you don't feed me?"

"If I recall, you're the one who decided to postpone dinner."

"I regarded this as more important." She reached for the veil. "Where's the kitchen?"

"Good Lord, don't you know you're supposed to be languid after sex?"

"Who made that rule? I feel *alive*. I want to go out and move mountains."

He looked at her glowing face and then smiled. "Not now. The mountains are a good hundred miles away. Stay where you are. I'll bring you something." He got out of bed and went toward the closet. "It's chilly and at least I have a robe to wear."

"I'm not cold."

He shrugged on the white terry robe. "No, you're not, thank God. I'll be back in a minute."

She watched the door close behind him before jumping out of bed and running to the closet. She grabbed a white shirt from a hanger and slipped it on. It came almost to her knees, but at least it covered her. She rifled through a bureau drawer and came up with a pair of white crew socks and pulled them on.

She padded out of the bedroom and wandered down the hall until she heard the sound of metal against metal and zeroed in on the kitchen. Gabe was standing in front of the stove pouring an egg mixture into a frying pan.

"Can I help?"

He glanced over his shoulder. "Don't you ever obey orders?"

"Not if I can help it. Besides, I'm too restless to sit still and be waited on."

His gaze traveled over her. "That shirt looks better on you than it does on me."

"Then it must look terrible on you." She made a face. "I hate cutesy outfits. They make me feel like Debbie Reynolds or Sandra Dee."

"What do you know about them? I'd think they'd be before your time."

"Are you kidding? The only movie theaters I got to go to when I was growing up were those in outback villages where Rudolph Valentino was still considered a current heartthrob." She moved to stand by his shoulder and peered down at the omelet. "That looks terrific. I'm so glad you can cook. I'm terrible at it. But I can make coffee," she offered.

"Then do it. The coffeemaker's on the counter over there. The coffee's in the canister." He took plates from a shelf in the cabinet and set them on the table. "I take it I'm going to do all the cooking while we're here."

"If you don't want chronic indigestion." She poured water into the coffeemaker. "Jed tried to teach me once, but he gave up. He says there's something seriously wrong with my culinary aptitude. I just don't have the gift. If you cook, I'll wash dishes."

"Sounds fair." With a spatula he lifted the omelet onto a plate, cut it neatly in half, and shifted one half to another plate. "Sit down and eat. You're going to need your strength later."

"Braggart." She could feel the heat in her cheeks as she sat down at the table. It was weird how he could make her blush when no one had been able to accomplish that feat in years. "You'd better be the one to shore up your reserves. I've decided I'm a nymphomaniac."

"Then you've decided wrong," he said quietly as he started to eat. "You're loving and sweet and passionate and I have bottomless reserves where you're concerned."

Her smile faded as she looked at him. "That's . . . nice."

"More than nice. Extraordinary. You're not eating." He looked up and smiled faintly. "Protein, remember."

"Sure I am." She picked up her fork and started on the omelet. "And you're the one who needs the protein." She had a sudden thought. "But you can't have any of that coffee. Why didn't you remind me before I started that pot? You need to sleep tonight."

"My dear, if I don't sleep tonight, I guarantee I'll never sleep again."

"No coffee," she said firmly.

He changed the subject. "What debt?"

She looked at him in confusion at the question that had come out of nowhere.

"I suppose there's no big secret now that you've told me everything else about your background." He paused before asking, "What debt did you owe me?"

"My life," she said simply. "Mekhit, Turkey, 1983."

He shook his head. "I was in Mekhit, but I—"

"You don't even remember. I didn't think you would. You dug me out of the ruins of a collapsed hotel after the earthquake. I knew I was only one of a score of people you helped during those two days, but you can understand why you were pretty prominent in my memory after that. You stayed with me and held my hand." She shivered even now at the memory. "It was the worst night of my life. The darkness—"

"Was like a coffin," he quoted. "I do remember. But your name was Anita."

"Anita Valdez. Spanish passport."

"And when we pulled you out . . ." His gaze went to her hair. "You were pretty messed up, but I'm sure your hair was dark."

"Vegetable dye. I had to look Spanish."

"I felt guilty about leaving you to go to the hospital alone."

"You did more than anyone could expect. The entire town was a disaster area. I knew you had to go and help dig out other people."

He grimaced. "You make me sound like Superman. I was only doing what anyone else would do in an emergency like that. I did drop by the hospital the day before I left Mekhit to see how you were."

"I didn't know that." She smiled radiantly. "That was nice of you."

"They said you disappeared after they bandaged your arm."

"Evan was there. He saw them put me in the ambulance and showed up at the emergency room to take me away. The deal had fallen through and we left Mekhit that night."

"To another deal . . . another country," he said bitterly.

"Yes." She finished her omelet and sat back in her chair. "But after that night I kept track of you. It wasn't hard. You were on the way up and were fairly visible." She chuckled. "And, in a way, I wasn't joking when I called you my Pygmalion. I first became interested in becoming a reporter because of you. I had a big-time crush on you for a long time and thought everything you did was the cat's pajamas."

He made a face. "Where on earth do you come up with those archaic expressions?"

"I like them. The twenties slang was very colorful. Bee's knees, cat's pajamas . . ."

"I'm beginning to like them myself. They suit you." He put down his fork, met her gaze, and said with deliberate emphasis, "But not as much as I suit you. To use one of your phrases, we fit like the cat's pajamas. Maybe that's why we were brought together at Mekhit."

"Don't tell me you believe in fate too?" she scoffed. "First tradition and now fate?"

"Why not? I do believe some people are meant to be together," he said softly. "And if you get lucky enough to find that person, you'd be stupid to let them go."

She would hold on forever.

She had believed in fate that night. She had found something strong and sure and unshakable in that volatile world. But the resolution she had made in Mekhit must be broken. By clinging to him to complete herself, she could hurt him.

"Cripes, you're sentimental," she said. "But I can't totally knock this togetherness bit. You really know how to show a girl a good time." She stood up and swaggered toward the door. "Dump the dishes in the sink. I'll do them in the morning. I have enough protein in me now to keep you interested for a while." She slanted him a stern glance over her shoulder. "And don't you dare touch that coffee."

"You didn't sleep again," Ronnie accused as she strolled with Gabe in the garden the next morning after breakfast. "So much for me exhausting you."

"I dozed a little," Gabe said.

She gazed at him worriedly. "You don't look it. I think you're just saying that to keep me from nagging you."

"It's entirely possible. You're persistent enough to make a saint try misdirection." He shot her a glance. "And very caring for a woman who only wants my body."

"I do care about you." She looked away from him. "I told you I liked you. You're not stupid enough to believe I'd have sex with a man I didn't like."

"No, you wouldn't tell me such an arrant lie. Because you're not stupid either." His hand closed on hers. "Though I've noticed a distinct muddleheadedness on occasion."

"We're talking about you."

"In connection with you." He stopped beside a white net hammock stretched between two pepper trees. "*Vive la connexion*. Would you care to forge another link? I've never done it in a hammock before."

He was deftly changing the subject in a manner he knew would appeal to her, Ronnie thought in exasperation. It was a smart move. She had never dreamed she had such a sensual nature until last night. "This isn't about sex." She turned to face him. "Call Dan and ask him to bring sleeping pills when he comes tonight."

"No pills." He sat down on the hammock and pulled her down beside him. "Read my lips, Ronnie. I don't take pills. I've seen too many people start out taking a few pills to relieve tension and end up hooked. People whom I respect for their strength and good sense."

"But you can't—" There was no use arguing with him. He wasn't going to change his mind. She would have to go about seeking a solution indirectly. The only problem was that indirectness was not her forte. She lay down in the hammock and pulled him down beside her. "Okay, I'll drop it. What do I care if you turn into an insomniac? All the better for me. I'll just reach over in the middle of the night and know you're always ready for play."

"Then shall we try the hammock?"

"Not now. Later." She cuddled closer and put her head on his shoulder. "I like this little garden. Someday I'd like to have a garden of my own."

"I'll give you this one."

"It wouldn't be the same. I think you have to plan and work in a garden to make it your own."

"Like any endeavor."

"Right." She chuckled. "Like setting up an angle for a camera shoot. I have a whole garden of photos that I've planted over the— Why are you frowning?"

"The sun's too bright. I hate bright li—" He broke off and then asked, "What would you plant in your garden?"

She went still. He had caught himself too quickly and the change of subject had come with equal swiftness.

Bright light.

He had said she wasn't stupid, but she had been blind. When she had been imprisoned in Kuwait, glaring light as well as darkness had been used to torture prisoners, to keep them awake, to shred their nerves and weaken their resolve. "How long . . . did they do it to you?"

He didn't try to lie. He knew she wouldn't believe him. "The first six weeks."

Six weeks bathed in light, not permitted to sleep. "You didn't say anything about it at the news conference."

"It was no big deal."

She knew better. It was a very big deal. "You let me have the light on that night at Fatima's. No wonder you didn't sleep."

"I probably wouldn't have slept anyway. I told you, it was an aftereffect."

"You don't know. It might have triggered something that caused you not to sleep again. For heaven's sake, you should have told me."

"You had your own demons. I'm not afraid of the light, it just bothers me."

"Dammit, you'd just gotten away from those bastards. I could have stood the dark, but no, you had to prove what a big, strong man you are."

"Stop crying."

"I'm not crying."

"Then why are you getting my shirt wet?" His hand gently stroked the hair at her temple.

He was comforting her again, blast it. He was the one who needed help and comfort and she was bawling on his chest. She wiped her wet cheeks on the front of his shirt. "Serves you right." She pulled his head down on her breast so that his eyes were shaded by the shadows of the branches overhead, and held him passionately close. "I want to kill them."

"I'm the one you're killing. I'm about to smother in your delightful bosom." His lips brushed the cleavage revealed by the shirt. "Though I couldn't imagine a nicer death."

She loosened her grip but still kept him close. "Shut up. I don't want you to talk. I want to hold you."

"I hear and obey." His long body relaxed against her. "Actually, after a year of deprivation, I could use some tender loving care."

"Then be quiet and enjoy it." Her hand stroked his hair. She said unsteadily, "You're such a fool."

"Is that any way to talk to Daddy Warbucks?" he murmured. "And every fool should have the luck to land in a spot like this."

She didn't answer. She could hear the sound of the birds and feel the rise and fall of his breathing against her breasts. The scent of the flowers was all around them and the breeze was a soothing caress. She sensed the tension slowly, gradually, seep out of him.

Fifteen minutes later he fell into a light doze.

Forty minutes later he drifted from that state into a deep sleep.

One leg was thrown over her and the weight of his heavy body was holding her perfectly immobile, but she didn't try to move. She was almost afraid to breathe. She lay there as the afternoon sunlight faded into twilight and then to the darkness of evening.

• • •

"Ronnie."

She opened her eyes at the soft call to see a tall figure silhouetted by the moonlight.

Dan Bredlowe squatted down beside the hammock. "I knocked and no one came to the door. Is everything all right?"

Gabe answered for her. "Fine." He stretched and then sat up. "I guess I must have fallen asleep." He turned to look at Ronnie. "You make a great pillow."

"Better than pills?"

"Much better than pills." He leaned down and kissed her forehead. "Come on, I'll see if I can stir up something for Dan to eat."

She shook her head. "You go on. I'll be there as soon as I wake up a little."

His gaze narrowed curiously on her face but he rose to his feet and sauntered back toward the house with Dan.

She waited until he reached the French doors before she started to move. Lord, she was cramped and stiff in every muscle and one leg was asleep. She managed to get to her feet after two tries, but only managed to hobble down the path, dragging one leg behind her.

"You look like the hunchback of Notre Dame." Gabe stood in the doorway watching her. "Did I do that to you?"

"No, I did it to myself. I should have moved."

"But you didn't want to wake me."

"I fell asleep myself." She grabbed hold of the doorway. The leg that was asleep was beginning to tingle. "Where's Dan?"

"I sent him to bring in your luggage from the helicopter. I thought it strange you didn't come with us. You have too much energy to enjoy lolling in hammocks." He slipped his arm around her waist. "Foot asleep?"

"The whole leg, but it's coming back. You don't have to help me."

"It's my privilege." The words were only half-mocking. "Lean on me."

She let him have a little of her weight as she released the door and took a step into the living room. "Stop pampering me. It's not necessary."

"No, and it wasn't necessary for you to lie there for over eight hours with my bulk on you." He drew her closer. "It's just the kind of thing people do when they love each other."

"I don't—"

"Give me more of your weight," he interrupted. "It's not going to compromise your independence to admit to weakness. As soon as we get to the kitchen, you can sit down and supervise my cooking." He raised a brow. "Unless you care to give it a try yourself."

She shook her head. "We need Dan to bring us news. You don't want him incapacitated for any length of time." They had reached the kitchen and she frowned as Gabe flipped on the light. She hadn't realized last night how brilliant were the recessed halogen lights in the ceiling. "They're too bright."

"What do you want to do? Dine by candle-light?" He seated her in one of the chairs at the table. "For Lord's sake, I'm beginning to regret that slip of the tongue. You're going overboard. I'm not that sensitive."

He wouldn't admit it if he was. She would have to do something about those lights. "You should have told me before."

"Should have told you what?" Dan strolled into the kitchen. "Secrets already in this Shangri-la of marital bliss?"

Ronnie grinned. "He should have told me he could cook. It would have given me an even greater incentive to get him out of Said Ababa." She leaned back in her chair and waved a hand airily. "Cook, slave."

EIGHT

Dan finished his casserole and leaned back in his chair. "A repast for the gods. Good job, Gabe."

"It's nice to be appreciated." He slanted a glance at Ronnie. "May I offer the man a cup of coffee?"

"As long as you don't have one yourself." She got up, went to the refrigerator, and took out a gallon of milk. "Dan, bring some decaffeinated coffee when you come next time." She poured a glass of milk and brought it to Gabe. "Gabe's having a little trouble sleeping."

"What a nag," Gabe said as he sipped the milk.

She took Dan's cup to the coffeemaker on the counter, poured out the hot liquid, and after giving it to him, sat back down. "Nagging is sensible when dealing with unsensible human beings."

Dan chuckled. "Good God, you two sound like you've been married ten years. Pilsner might get off your back if he could hear you now."

Ronnie involuntarily tensed at the name. She realized with a sense of shock that the scene with Pilsner had taken place only yesterday. So much had happened since that interview on the terrace, it might have occurred a year ago.

"How much damage did he do?" Gabe asked.

Dan looked at him in surprise. "Didn't you see him on television? The story has been all over the networks."

"We haven't turned on the set," Gabe said. "How bad?"

Dan shrugged. "Not good. Pilsner's very credible, very upright, and doesn't come across as your typical bureaucrat."

"He's a patriot, not a bureaucrat," Ronnie said quietly.

Gabe ignored her. "Have you heard from Koras?"

"He's doing all he can but Pilsner's well respected in the administration. The news media is on your side and public opinion is rallying."

"Keep the pressure on. I want everything

done that can be done to undermine Pilsner's position."

"No," Ronnie said. "Leave Pilsner alone."

"We can't leave him alone," Gabe said impatiently. "He's the key."

"Then it's a key we won't use," Ronnie said. "No slanted stories. No digging into his past to discredit him."

"He's trying hard enough to discredit you," Dan said. "He's had to defend himself, so he's pouncing on your background with both feet."

"I deserve it. He doesn't."

Dan looked at Gabe. "You're the boss. What do I do?"

"No, Gabe," Ronnie said.

He opened his mouth to argue with her and then closed it again. "Put it on hold, Dan," he said finally. "I'll get back to you later. Keep on issuing positive stories. Rehash the wedding. Make sure Koras is kept primed."

Dan nodded as he rose to his feet. "I'll keep you informed. I guess I'd better get back to Marasef."

"You could stay the night," Ronnie offered.

He shook his head. "Far be it from me to interrupt a honeymoon." He hesitated before he said to Ronnie, "Look, Pilsner's making some pretty grim noises. He'd throw the book at you if he got the chance."

"You already told me that." Ronnie smiled. "Duly noted."

"I just don't want you to make any mistakes. You're safe here, but leave Sedikhan and you're in trouble."

He was saying that Sedikhan was a prison for her . . . and for Gabe if he chose to stay with her.

"She's not budging," Gabe said. "Where else would she get someone to cook for her?"

Dan chuckled, his expression lightening. "Yeah, I knew you had some use. John has a few business decisions he'd like you to make. Is it all right if I have him call you here?"

Gabe shook his head. "I'll call him."

"Whatever you say." Dan gave them both a casual wave and strolled out of the kitchen.

Gabe turned to her and attacked as soon as Dan left the room. "Stop putting blocks in my way. For Lord's sake, don't you want to win?"

"You don't know how much."

"Then we have to get Pilsner before he gets you, dammit."

"You wouldn't go after him if it wasn't for

me. He's one of the good guys." She smiled without mirth. "And there are too few of them in Washington to waste. Somewhere along the way the politicians forgot what they're supposed to be doing up there."

Gabe's expression froze. "We the people?"

She nodded. "Do you know, I didn't have a formal education until I left Evan. We were always traveling and on the run, so I picked up what I could from correspondence courses and any books I came across. One of my favorite was a dog-eared volume of American history for children. It was full of things like Pilgrims and Indians at the first Thanksgiving and Betsy Ross sewing a flag and Nathan Hale dying for his country. A lot of those stories were pure fiction and pretty schmaltzy, but I believed them. I guess I still believe them."

Gabe smiled resignedly. "I think you do, heaven help you."

"Maybe heaven will help me." She smiled with an effort. "But it won't if we shoot down the good guys. So back off Pilsner."

He shook his head. "You're making a mistake."

"But you'll do as I say?"

"I'm not promising anything. I'll try to find

another way, but I won't have you sacrificed to Pilsner's standard of right and wrong."

It was the only commitment she was going to get from him, but the delay might be enough. There would be no reason to pursue Pilsner if she was not around to benefit.

She stood up and began stacking the dishes. "Why don't you find a deck of cards while I do these dishes? I don't think either of us is going to sleep any more tonight."

"May I ask what you're doing?" Gabe asked from the doorway of the kitchen a week later. He quickly strode forward to steady the ladder on which she was balancing.

"I'm shading these light bulbs with pink tissue paper." She glanced down at him with a grin. "Pretty romantic, huh?"

"You wish to arouse my libido in the kitchen?" Gabe asked. "My cooking must be getting pretty boring."

"Once I saw a television show that featured a sex therapist who said every couple should make love in unconventional places." She finished taping the paper and started down the ladder. "I want to be prepared."

"You refused the hammock. What could be more unusual than that?"

"Try me tonight, by the light of the moon. I howl at midnight."

"You do? That should be interesting." He regarded the pink tissue paper. "Do you realize there's every chance that paper will catch fire if the lights are left on too long?"

"We'll be careful," she said cheerfully. "It's only temporary. I'm going to phone Dan and tell him to bring a whole box of pink light bulbs next time he comes."

"Because pink is soft and there won't be glare." He shook his head, but his smile was tender. "Why not red lights?"

"I thought red would be a bit surreal. Pink is fine. Pink is good."

"No, it's Ronnie who is fine." He reached forward to kiss her on the lips. "All this isn't necessary, you know. It was only a temporary thing."

"Maybe. We won't take any chances."

"I believe I like you in this maternal mode." He slipped an arm around her and led her out of the kitchen. "What do you have planned for the bedroom?"

"Nothing maternal." Her smile faded as the full import of her words sank home to her. "And that reminds me. I want you to start protecting me."

"I'd say you're a little late," Gabe said dryly.

"Since we've been intimate in the extreme for the last week."

"Better late than never. It didn't occur to me." A possibility existed that she had been deliberately irresponsible. Perhaps she had wanted to have Gabe's baby. "I'm not alone in this. You should have thought about it too."

"I assumed you were on the Pill." His rare, warm smile lit his face. "A baby . . ."

"No," she said quickly. "Don't even think about it." She was thinking far too much about it herself. She had never thought of herself as maternal, but she knew she would want Gabe's baby even though it would complicate her life enormously.

"I can't help it. It intrigues me."

"Forget it. If I got pregnant . . ."

He went still. "You'd abort?"

She shook her head. "That wouldn't be my choice."

"Thank God. I was afraid I'd have to kidnap you and hold you prisoner until I could talk you into keeping it."

"For goodness sake, why are we talking about

this? I'm probably not pregnant, and from now on you protect me. Right?"

"Right." His smile deepened. "I protect you. It's a role that suits me to a tee."

She felt a flicker of despair. There it was again. Protection. Responsibility. They were growing closer every day, every hour, and Gabe's natural instinct was to guard anything and anyone he cared about. She had reached out to grab happiness for herself and Gabe was being caught in the trap.

"Stop frowning." With an index finger he traced the wrinkle that furrowed her brow. "I can practically see the wheels turning beneath those blond curls. It's your body. If you don't want a child right now, that's fine with me. I just wanted you to know that I'd want your child anytime, anywhere."

"Thanks," she said, emotion making her voice husky.

"You're welcome." Gabe bowed with mock politeness. "Just so you know I'm willing to oblige."

"I know." Her hand closed tightly around his. He had just gotten out of one prison and would oblige her to the point of making himself a prisoner again in lovely Tanadahl. "I've always found you very accommodating."

• • •

Dan arrived at Tanadahl at noon the next day. Ronnie ran out to the helicopter to meet him. "You're early. We didn't expect you until dinnertime. Did you bring my light—" For the first time she noticed the gravity of his expression. "What's wrong?"

He didn't answer. "Where's Gabe?" he asked as he jumped out of the helicopter

"In the study. He's trying to wade through some of that paperwork you brought last time." She searched his expression. "Is it Pilsner?"

He gently took her arm and propelled her toward the house. "I think we should wait until Gabe is present."

"I'm here." Gabe came down the front steps. "What's happened?"

"It's Ronnie's father. He's been shot."

Gabe muttered a curse as he came swiftly down the steps to stand beside Ronnie. "The Red December?"

Dan shook his head. "It happened in Tamrovia. He was dealing with a dissident group for arms and was caught in a raid by the Tamrovian authorities."

"How bad?"

"Critical." Dan turned to Ronnie and said gently, "They don't think he'll make it. I can't tell you how sorry I am to bring you this news."

"Are you sure?" she asked numbly. She couldn't believe that Evan was hurt, perhaps dying. He was one of those people who sailed through life. People around him got hurt, but never Evan.

Dan nodded. "Our sources in Belsen are very reliable. It took the Tamrovians a little while to identify him. He was traveling with an Irish passport under the name Robert Reardon."

"Where is he?"

"Being guarded at a hospital in Belsen, Tamrovia."

"Will you take me there in the helicopter?"

Dan looked at Gabe.

"How public is this information?" Gabe asked.

"It's our story so far, but it could break anytime."

Gabe turned to Ronnie. "Can I point out a few hard facts without upsetting you?" he asked quietly.

"Probably not."

"I have to do it anyway." He slipped his arms around her. "It could be a dangerous move for you. The minute you cross the Sedikhan border, you're leaving yourself vulnerable to Pilsner. If we know about your father, then you can bet Pilsner will soon. It's a five-hour flight to Tamrovia. There may be a watch at the hospital by the time we get there."

"I'm not stupid enough not to guess that."

"You don't owe your father anything. He used you."

"I used him too. I tried to talk him out of arms running, but when he only laughed at me, I used his contacts, I followed him into a dozen hot spots to get stories."

"He brought you up like a ragtag gypsy."

"He did what he could."

"To make you a criminal like him. You don't *owe* him, Ronnie."

Evan, who had never believed in sentiment or obligation, would have been the first to agree with him, she thought sadly. But she had never been like Evan, and loving Gabe had made her willing to admit to herself how desperately she had wanted to know and love her father. This might be her last chance. "I don't know if I owe him anything for being my father, but I owe him for Said Ababa," she said unevenly. "He helped me save you. I have to see him, Gabe. I can't let him die alone." She stepped back out of his arms and turned to Dan. "Will you take me or do I go on my own?"

"We'll take you," Gabe said. "Go in and pack a bag for us while I talk to Dan about arrangements for the trip."

"What arrangements?"

"You don't have a passport. We'll have to enter Tamrovia illegally."

"That will be a first for you." She wearily shook her head. "This is my problem. I shouldn't involve you in all this."

"You couldn't keep me out of it." He pushed her gently toward the door. "Try to hurry. The sooner we get there, the better off we'll be."

The helicopter landed in a field a few miles outside Belsen, where a car and driver were waiting to take them to the hospital in the city.

"I'm making you a criminal too," Ronnie said as she watched the scenery flash by the window.

"I doubt if they'll deport me for helping my wife get to her dying father." Gabe's hand closed on hers. "Lord, your muscles are stiff as boards."

"I need to *get* there."

"I know it's seemed like a long trip, but we're

almost there. It should take about fifteen minutes to get to the hospital."

"Will they let me see him?"

He nodded. "I had Dan radio ahead. Our local station manager set it up."

"Thank you. I'm sorry to be so much trouble." She was silent a moment, and when she spoke again it was in a barely audible voice. "It isn't that I owe him. He's . . . alone, Gabe. He's always been on the fringe. He never let anyone close to him. I lived with him for eighteen years and he never let even me get close. He's so alone."

"Which made you pretty damn alone too."

"I don't think he could help it. Some people can't. I wanted him to love me, but maybe there was something lacking in him." She moistened her lips. "Maybe he didn't have the aptitude. You know, like I can't cook?"

His only answer was the tightening of his hand holding hers.

"I still can't believe this. He never thought he could be hurt. He said he had nine lives. . . ."

They pulled up in front of the hospital a short time later. "Dan, go see Harry Spaulding and set up those arrangements I told you about and then come right back to the hospital," Gabe said as he helped her out of the car. His grip was a warm support beneath her elbow as they made their way through the lobby to the bank of elevators. "It's room seven-twelve. We'll have to get clearance at the nurses' station before you'll be allowed in."

A few minutes later they were on the seventh floor and moving down the hall toward the nurses' station.

A plump, dark-haired nurse checked the chart. "Your name's on the list, but I'll have to see identification."

"How is he?" Ronnie asked.

"He's unconscious." The nurse handed back their identification. "You'll have to ask the doctor for any further information. He'll be making his rounds in another hour. Follow me." She got up and moved quickly down the corridor on silent white-shod feet.

A uniformed guard stopped them at the door, but at the nurse's nod he permitted Ronnie and Gabe to enter the room.

The room looked like all hospital rooms, sterile and pristine and without character. The scent was also the same—antiseptic and astringent. Only the man lying in the white-sheeted bed was an anomaly. Evan didn't belong here.

He shouldn't be in a hospital; he had nine lives.

"Evan?" she whispered.

He was going to die.

The certainty came to her as she looked at him. She had not believed it until this moment, but she had seen men on the verge of death before and Evan was very close.

Gabe could see it too. His hand tightened on her arm as he felt the shiver that went through her. "Okay?"

She nodded.

He got her the only visitors' chair in the room and set it beside the bed. "Sit down. I'll go get another chair for myself from the nurse."

"No, don't stay. I'll be all right." She sat down, her gaze on Evan's pale face. "Leave me alone with him."

"Are you sure?"

"He's never met you. You're a stranger to him. He was surrounded by strangers all of his life. I don't want him to—" She broke off and steadied her voice. "Wait for me outside."

He nodded and left the room.

She kept vigil all night and was vaguely conscious of Gabe bringing her a pillow, a cup of coffee, sometimes just standing beside her for a moment, his hand on her shoulder to let her know he was there.

It was close to four in the morning when he appeared again at her elbow. "The story has broken. The corridor is a mob scene of reporters." He paused. "And Pilsner's here."

She couldn't worry about Pilsner now. "We expected it, didn't we?"

He nodded. "There's no way I'm going to let him in here, but I thought you ought to know." He looked at Evan's still form. "I didn't want it to come as a shock when you left the room."

He meant when Evan died.

"Has he regained consciousness at all?" Gabe asked.

She shook her head.

"I spoke to the doctor. He may not."

"I don't care. No one is certain how much awareness people have in a coma. He could know I'm here."

Gabe nodded and left the room

Evan stirred a little before dawn. His lids fluttered and then slowly opened and focused on her face. For a moment she thought he didn't recognize her, but then he said, "Mushy . . . always . . . were."

"You told me it was one of my failings."

His smile was the sardonic one she knew so well. "Came running . . . to my . . . deathbed."

He knew he was going to die. She wouldn't insult him by denying it. She nodded jerkily.

"I . . . wouldn't have come to . . . yours."

She swallowed. "I think you would."

He looked at her and a flicker of expression crossed his face. "Maybe . . ."

He lapsed back into unconsciousness and died a few minutes later.

Maybe.

She sat there looking at him. "You would have come, Evan," she whispered fiercely. "Why couldn't you say it? Blast you, I *know* you would have come."

The tears she had held back were suddenly flowing down her cheeks as she stood up and walked stiffly to the door.

Gabe.

She had to get to Gabe.

NINE

Gabe came to her the minute she appeared in the hall. He took one look at her tear-stained face and enveloped her in his arms. Lord, how she needed him now. Warmth. Safety. Life.

"He's gone?" he asked in a low voice.

She nodded. "A few minutes ago. I can't stop crying. Evan would have hated it. . . ." She was vaguely conscious that the hall was full of people, cameras, lights. She looked over Gabe's shoulder and saw Pilsner standing across the corridor, a uniformed guard by his side. She smiled crookedly. "Hello, Mr. Pilsner. Sorry to keep you waiting."

He nodded. "I'm genuinely sorry that I have to intrude on such an unhappy occasion." He wasn't being untruthful; he was genuinely sympathetic, but it wouldn't keep him from doing what he believed was right.

Gabe thrust a handkerchief into her hand. "Go to the rest room and wash your face with cold water. It will make you feel better. I'll go to the nurses' station and make the arrangements for Evan."

"Cremation," she said. "He hated funerals."

"Let me handle it." He turned her around and gave her a push down the hall. "It's the last door before you reach the turn in the corridor. I'll be here when you get back." He turned to stare challengingly at Pilsner. "I assume that's all right with you?" he asked.

Pilsner hesitated and then nodded to the guard. "Wait outside for her. Keep those reporters out of there and off her back."

That was nice of him, she thought dully as she entered the rest room. He was probably a very kind man when his job wasn't involved, the home type who barbecued for the wife and kids every weekend.

The bathroom was deserted, thank heavens. She passed a row of stalls with half-open doors and stopped at the basins at the end of the room. The mirrors reflected an outer image that looked as bad as she felt inside—tousled hair and red swollen eyes, tear-streaked cheeks. Dammit, why couldn't she stop crying? She started splashing cold water on her face.

"Ronnie."

She jumped and whirled to see a man coming out of one of the stalls. "Dan!"

"Come on. We haven't got much time." He gestured to an oak door to the left of the basins. "That door connects with the men's rest room. I broke the lock earlier."

"You want me to go into the men's room?"

"The entrance to the men's room is around the corner of the corridor." He pushed her through the door and slammed it behind them, then pulled her past a row of urinals. "Look, I know you're in shock, but just let me lead you. Okay?"

She wasn't capable of doing anything else at the moment.

He glanced cautiously out the door into the corridor and then said, "Come on." He dragged her at a half run down the corridor toward the emergency exit and down the steps to the sixth floor. "We'll take the elevator from this floor. It's faster than the stairs." As he ushered her into the elevator he said. "There's a car waiting outside to take us to the helicopter."

"You planned all this?"

"Gabe planned it. There was no way he was going to let Pilsner grab you." He made a face. "Though I take credit for spending two very uncomfortable hours in that toilet stall ducking a stream of ladies while I was waiting for you to appear."

The elevator doors opened and he ushered her quickly through the lobby to the car waiting at the curb.

"Gabe figures it will be at least fifteen minutes before they send someone in to check on you." He glanced at his watch. "That gives us ten to get out of the city." He motioned to the driver to go as he got into the car beside her. "Gabe will stall them as long as he can, but when Pilsner starts getting nervous, he'll slip away." He stared at her pale face. "Are you taking any of this in?"

She nodded. "How will Gabe get to the helicopter?"

"There's another car around the corner and two blocks down the street. We were afraid the timing would be too close for him to have it wait in front of the hospital. He didn't want to be followed to the helicopter." He smiled gently. "Don't worry, we've got it all covered. You'll be back in Tanadahl in no time and Pilsner will be wiping egg off his face."

• • •

Gabe arrived at the helicopter thirty minutes after Dan and Ronnie, and by that time she had emerged from her emotional stupor enough to be worried at the delay and very relieved at his appearance.

"How did it go?" Dan asked as Gabe climbed into the helicopter.

"I had no trouble evading Pilsner, but I had to run six blocks north and double back to get away from the reporters. Let's get out of here." As the helicopter lifted off Gabe asked Ronnie, "How do you feel?"

"I'm not sure. Everything has happened so fast."

"I had to get you out of there."

"I know. It's just . . ." She leaned back and closed her eyes. "Will you get into trouble?"

"We'll have to see. Pilsner wasn't pleased. We'll face that when we have to."

"I never meant to get you into trouble. I just had to see Evan."

"One good rescue deserves another, and any risk I ran was a drop in the bucket compared to what you did in Said Ababa." He loosened her seat belt and pulled her sideways to rest against his shoulder. "Try to sleep until we get back to Tanadahl."

She doubted if she could sleep, but she relaxed against him. She could hear the steady beat of his heart beneath her ear. He was all the comfort she had never had, the emotional safety Evan had never given her. He was an anchor that would hold steady through the years. Yet he was also excitement, passion, humor, and challenge. She could have it all.

If she was selfish enough to take it at his expense.

Evan had been that selfish. He had taken and never given. Not even in that last moment . . .

"Come on." Gabe lifted her out of the helicopter and half carried her across the courtyard. "You're out on your feet. Let's get you to bed."

"I don't want to be like him, Gabe," she murmured as she stumbled down the corridor toward their bedroom. "He always thought that he'd make a big stake that would set him up for life, the big bonanza. But he would still have been alone. Because he just took and never gave back."

He was quickly undressing her. "You're not like him."

"I hope not. I don't want to be alone."

"You'll never be alone." He slipped her beneath the sheets and lay down beside her, holding her. "I'll always be here."

"You didn't undress."

"Later." He brushed her hair back from her forehead. "I just want to hold you."

She wanted him to hold her. She wanted him to hold her and never, never let her go. . . .

When Ronnie awoke, Gabe was gone. She glanced at the clock on the bedside table and found she had slept for over twelve hours. It didn't surprise her. She had felt wounded both emotionally and bodily as she lay in Gabe's arms last night. She had not gone to sleep for a long time and had gradually felt the desolation seep out of her. Strange how Gabe could heal her, rid her of fear and unhappiness just by being there. He had first accomplished that magic in Mekhit, and since he had come back into her life, it had begun happening again.

She slowly got up and went to the bathroom. She felt sad and a little empty, but the shock of

Evan's death was gone, leaving only the resolution she had made before she went to sleep last night.

After showering and dressing she went in search of Gabe.

Dan was sitting at the kitchen table reading a newspaper. "Hi, you look better."

"I feel better. Where's Gabe?"

"I took him to Marasef to see the sheikh. He sent me back to take care of you." Dan grinned. "He didn't want you to starve to death. Would you like breakfast or lunch?"

"Just toast and coffee. Even I can make that."

"Sit down. I think you can stand a little pampering after what you went through yesterday."

"I put you and Gabe through a lot too," she said soberly. "I'm sorry, Dan. It was something I had to do."

"I know." He filled the coffeemaker. "Actually, it was kind of exciting. I haven't had that kind of action since I was a reporter covering Beirut."

"Will you get into trouble with the authorities?"

"Gabe says no." He put bread in the toaster. "You should see the coverage we got from your great escape. You've become a folk heroine. Pilsner's definitely shown in a bad light."

"But he won't give up." Pilsner had felt genuine sympathy for her at Belsen, but had not shifted in determination. This humiliation would only reinforce it. "He'll never give up."

Dan nodded. "He returned to Sedikhan last night. He's staying at a hotel in Marasef and trying to convince the sheikh to make an exception to his extradition policy and surrender you."

"What are the chances?"

"Not good. The sheikh and Gabe are good friends and His Majesty has an intense dislike of being pressured."

She made a face. "Cripes, I'm an international incident."

"Yep." He set the coffee and toast in front of her. "And I've never known a more interesting one," he said gently. "It's going to be fine, Ronnie."

"Yeah, sure," Ronnie said. "Except that Pilsner's been made to look foolish and he wants my head on a platter." It couldn't go on. The problems she had brought to Gabe were growing by leaps and bounds. "When is Gabe due back?"

"He said to tell you he'd be back in a few

hours. Dave's flying him here in the helicopter."
Dan looked at his watch. "Anytime now."

She finished the coffee and toast and stood
up. "When he gets here, will you tell Dave to
wait before he flies back to Marasef?"

Dan frowned. "Wait for what?"

"For me." She started toward the door. "I'm
going with him."

She was almost finished packing when Gabe
strode into the bedroom.

"What the hell do you think you're doing?"

"I'm leaving. What does it look like?" She
went to the closet, got her leather jacket, and
tossed it on the bed beside the open suitcase.
"It's over. Kaput."

He stood in the doorway and watched her as
she threw a pair of jeans into the suitcase. "You're
going to a great deal of trouble for nothing. I'm
not going to let you go."

"You have no choice in the matter. It's my
decision. Our relationship is history."

"Why?"

"Because that's the way I want it."

"Bull. Where are you going? You don't have
a passport."

"I have contacts. I can buy another passport on the black market."

"Not an American passport. You're too hot to handle."

"Then I'll buy a French or a Spanish or—" Her voice broke and she had to wait a minute before she could speak again. "You don't have to worry about me. I'll be fine. I'm not your responsibility."

"You *are* my responsibility," he said as he crossed the room toward her. "Just as I'm yours. That's the way it goes when you love someone."

"But I don't love you. How many times do I have to tell you? I don't—"

His hand covered her lips. "Hush. I'm getting pretty tired of that song and dance. You do love me. You're absolutely crazy about me, and if we're lucky, we're going to spend the next fifty years together."

"Lucky?" she repeated bitterly as she jerked away and slammed the suitcase shut. "Where are we going to spend those years? You'd grow to hate me. You don't know what it's like trying to survive on the fringe. I've lived there all my life and I'm not going to make you live there too."

"Because you love me too much?" Gabe asked softly.

She whirled to face him. "All right, because I love you too much," she said fiercely. "I love you! Are you satisfied?"

"No, I'd prefer for you to say it with a modicum of tenderness, but it will do for now."

"It doesn't make any difference if I love you or not. I'm leaving and I'm not coming back. You can file for a divorce and I'll—"

"No divorce. If you file, I'll fight it."

"Why?" she asked in despair. "Do you know what life would be like for you? I can't ever go back to America. That's where your roots are, your business holdings, your friends."

"I'm not saying I won't miss it." His hands cupped her shoulders. "But I'd miss you more. I won't give you up, Ronnie."

"You're going to have to."

He shook his head. "You've been so concerned with saving me from this dreaded 'fringe' that you've never bothered to consult me. You found that life terrible because you were made to feel so alone. We'll be together from now on."

Together. The word was as beautiful as a beacon in a storm. "You've never been there. You don't know."

"I know what you're like. I know what our life has been like this past week."

"Life can't always be a honeymoon."

"Who says? There's no reason why it can't if we work at it." He framed her face with his hands and looked into her eyes. "Listen, Ronnie, I've found something I've never had before. What I'm giving up is nothing to what I'm gaining."

Dear God, she loved him. He was saying the words she most wanted to hear and it was terribly painful to keep putting obstacles in his path. "It wouldn't work. Long-distance relationships never do. You'd have to spend three quarters of your time in the States attending to your business."

"I'd transfer the central office here."

"I'd get bored just staying here in Tanadahl and being a hausfrau. I'd turn into something you wouldn't like."

"Who wants you to be a hausfrau? We'll work it out. I talked to the sheikh this morning and he consented to grant you Sedikhan citizenship. That means you'll be eligible to receive a Sedikhan passport."

"A legal passport?" she asked, stunned.

"Very legal in the international community and backed by a heck of a lot of clout. We'd live here at Tanadahl and you'd be free to travel to pursue your career."

She shook her head. "Only to those countries

with no extradition treaties with the U.S."

He nodded. "That's true. I can't offer you the whole world. I wish I could." He asked softly, "Is this enough?"

It was enough for her, more than she had ever dreamed possible. It was a miracle. She hurled herself into his arms and buried her face in his chest. Her voice was muffled. "I shouldn't let you do it."

"You're not letting me do anything. You're just responding to an irresistible force."

"Geez, you're vain." Her arms tightened around him. She whispered, "I do love you."

"Louder."

She looked up at him. "I've loved you since the moment you took my hand in that ruin in Mekhit and I'll love you until the day I die."

His eyes glittered with moisture as he kissed her lips. "Now, that's a satisfactory declaration. I knew you'd get it right with a little practice."

"Better than yours," she said unsteadily. "But I admit offering to give up your country for me had a certain punch." She released him and stepped back. "Is Dave still waiting for me in the helicopter?"

He shook his head. "I wasn't taking any chances. I told him to go back to Marasef."

"Too bad. You'll have to radio him to come back."

He stiffened. "I thought we had settled this."

"A typical male assumption. You settled everything to your satisfaction but not to mine."

"Ronnie, for Lord's sake, this is—"

She stopped him with a quick kiss on the lips. "Shut up and call Dave. Don't worry, you're not going to get rid of me now. I just have something to do in Marasef."

"Are you sure you want to see him?" Gabe asked as they walked down the hotel corridor. "You've had enough traumas in the last forty-eight hours. You don't need the flak he's going to give you."

"I don't expect a warm, social meeting. It's just something I have to do."

She knocked on the door of Pilsner's room.

Pilsner's expression was impassive as he opened the door. "Good day, Mrs. Falkner. I was surprised to receive your phone call. Won't you come in?"

"Thank you. It's kind of you to see me."

"I assure you, I don't feel in a kindly mood." He closed the door after they entered. "I won't offer you any refreshments, as I assume this will be a very short visit." He glanced coldly at Gabe. "I wasn't pleased with that trickery at the hospital."

"I wasn't pleased with you for trying to jail my wife. I happen to like having her around."

"I was doing my duty."

"Stop squabbling," Ronnie wearily told them both. "I'm sorry, Mr. Pilsner, Gabe is being very protective of me these days."

"I've noticed that," he said coldly. "He's made my position in this matter very uncomfortable."

Gabe said, "Believe me, it could have been worse."

"I realize that," Pilsner said to Ronnie's surprise. "I've been wondering at your restraint."

"Ronnie thinks you're Nathan Hale," Gabe said. "No below-the-belt punches to sterling patriots."

"Really?" A curious expression flickered over his face as he glanced at Ronnie. "How interesting."

"I knew I shouldn't have brought you, Gabe," she said impatiently. "May I speak now?"

"By all means," Pilsner said. "Let's get it over with."

"I'll make this as brief as I can." She took a

deep breath. "Your visit here is useless. You're not going to be able to touch me while I'm in Sedikhan. The sheikh has agreed to give me Sedikhan citizenship."

Pilsner's lips tightened. "Your doing, I assume, Falkner."

"Checkmate," Gabe said.

"No, it isn't," Ronnie said. "It's not really a victory for us. My husband would be giving up too much for me to accept. Sedikhan is a wonderful country, but it's not Gabe's country." She paused. "And it's not my country."

"You have no country," Pilsner said. "I'd think you'd be very glad of this opportunity. I doubt you'll get a better chance."

"Unless you offer me one."

His expression hardened. "I've told you that possibility doesn't exist."

"I have a deal to offer you."

"I don't make deals."

"Don't bristle, just listen to me. I'm not offering you a bribe." She took a deep breath. "Gabe is going to let the publicity about me die down and take the heat off you."

Gabe looked at her in shock. "The hell I am."

She ignored him. "If I let you take me back to

the States to stand trial, I doubt if any jury would give me more than five years. There's a good chance I'd get less, maybe even probation."

"You're not going to stand trial," Gabe said.

"You see, he'd do everything he could to make it easier for me. He's a very powerful and determined man." She added simply, "And he loves me."

"That's become abundantly clear to me," Pilsner said dryly. "Perhaps the marriage wasn't as contrived as I first thought, but it doesn't change anything. The crime still exists."

"I'll pay for it. I'll serve my probation in Sedikhan. I'll stay here for the next five years, and at the end of that time, if you don't agree I'm worthy of being an American citizen, I'll come back to the U.S. and give myself into your custody."

"No!" Gabe said.

"Is it a deal?" she asked Pilsner.

"It appears to be an arrangement slanted in my favor," he said cautiously. "All I have to do is wait."

"No, you also have to be fair. You have to keep an eagle eye on me, and if I make a false step, you give me a black mark. If I do something you like, you give me a gold star." She paused.

"And if you think I can contribute, if you think I'm worthy, maybe you'll let me come home."

"It's not likely."

"Is it a deal?"

"I have nothing to lose." There was a hint of sympathy in his expression as he added, "And you have everything to lose."

"So did those people back in 1776. Sometimes it's worth the risk if the prize is big enough." She turned and walked toward the door. "Come on, Gabe, I have to start gathering gold stars."

"Mrs. Falkner."

She turned to see Pilsner staring at her with a frown furrowing his high brow. "This is very difficult for me. I don't believe it's possible for you to convince me. One exception opens the floodgates. I can't set a precedent."

"Sure you can. Read your history books. America thrives on setting precedents." She opened the door. "And on second chances. That's the reason the Pilgrims came to Plymouth, and look what it says on the Statue of Liberty. That's all I'm asking." She smiled tremulously at him. "A second chance."

She didn't wait for an answer.

"You meant it, didn't you?" Gabe asked as he walked with her down the hall. "You intend to give yourself up if he doesn't come through."

"Yes, one way or another we're going home." She tucked her arm in his. "Even if it means you have to visit me every Sunday in the hoosegow on the Hudson."

"It's a big risk. He's one tough customer. It's always hard to deal with people who think they're in the right."

"We'll just have to prove him wrong. He's already made one mistake. He said I was risking everything." She smiled lovingly up at him. "*You're* everything. I've tried my darnedest, but you're too stubborn to let me lose you."

"You bet I am."

"Well, since I have everything, I just need the proper setting to put it in."

EPILOGUE

"Ronnie! Where the devil are you?"

"In the kitchen," she called. "And stop shouting. I'm trying to get this blasted cake to rise."

Gabe came into the kitchen. "You're cooking?" he asked warily.

"Last week I interviewed the chef at that four-star restaurant in Marasef and he said anyone could cook if they concentrate. He says he uses meditation to enhance his creations."

"And that makes the cake rise?"

"Well, I figured it couldn't hurt."

"Do I have to eat it?" he asked uneasily.

"It would be supportive." She peered through the glass oven door. "It's not doing anything. Why are you home early? I thought you said you were lunching with the sheikh."

"I got a call at the office and I canceled it." He paused. "The call was from Pilsner."

She tensed, her glance flying to the calendar on the wall. "I've got another eight months. He can't change my deadline."

Gabe nodded solemnly. "He's doing it. He says it's a foolish waste of time to continue with this campaign of yours. He wants me to personally escort you to Miami for trial."

"What?"

"Got you!" Gabe laughed and picked her up and whirled her in a circle. "No way."

Excitement soared through her. "I'm going to murder you. What did he really say?"

"He just got the news about the Emmy they gave you on the story about illegal aliens. He said the story was slanted and overly sentimental."

That didn't sound promising. "It was the truth and darned good investigative reporting."

"He's tired of receiving reports on your charity work with UNICEF."

"They're embarrassing to me, too, but how else can you get gold stars?"

"He said having to handle those thousands of petitions from people asking that you receive amnesty and be made a citizen was causing his entire staff to threaten to quit."

"Gabe!"

"He said you're the most persistent woman on the face of the earth. I agreed with him. He also said you're a nag without equal in the—"

"*Tell* me," she interrupted.

"He said if he didn't give in, he was sure you'd discover the cure for all known killer diseases plaguing mankind just to make him look bad."

She held her breath. "And?"

He reached into his pocket and pulled out a black velvet jeweler's box. "He said to be sure and give you this."

"He sent me a present?"

"Well, it's really from me."

She opened the box. An exquisite pearl choker with channel-set rubies and sapphires glittered on a bed of black velvet.

I thought the theme was fitting for a Star-Spangled Bride.

I'll give you the matching necklace when you become a citizen.

The words Gabe had spoken when he had given her the red, white, and blue earrings on their wedding day five years ago came back to her now.

She looked up eagerly from the necklace and the answer was in his face.

He said the words anyway. "We're going home, love."

THE EDITOR'S
CORNER

July belongs to ONLY DADDY—and six magnificent heroes who discover romance, family style! Whether he's a confirmed bachelor or a single father, a small-town farmer or a big-city cop, each of these men can't resist the pitter-patter of little feet. And when he falls under the spell of that special woman's charms, he'll stop at nothing to claim her as a partner in parenting and passion. . . .

Leading the terrific line-up for July is Linda Cajio with **ME AND MRS. JONES**, LOVESWEPT #624. Actually, it should be *ex*-Mrs. Jones since high school sweethearts Kate Perry and Mitch Jones have been divorced for eleven years, after an elopement and a disastrous brief marriage. Now Kate is back in town, and Mitch, who's always been able to talk her into just about anything, persuades her to adopt a wise-eyed injured tomcat, with the promise that he'd be making plenty of house calls! Not sure she can play stepmother to his daughter Chelsea, Kate tells herself to run from the man who so easily ignites her desire, but she still remembers his hands on her body and can't send him away. To Mitch, no memory can ever match the heat of their passion, and he's been waiting all this time to reclaim the only woman he's ever truly loved. With fire in his touch, he sets about convincing her to let him in once more, and this time he intends to keep her in his arms for always. An utterly delightful story from beginning to end, told with Linda's delicious sense of humor and sensitive touch.

In **RAISING HARRY**, LOVESWEPT #625 by Victoria Leigh, Griff Ross is a single father coping with the usual problems of raising a high-spirited three-year-old son. He's never been jealous of Harry until he finds him in the arms of their neighbor Sharron Capwell. Her lush mouth makes Griff long to kiss her breathless, while her soft curves tempt him with visions of bare shoulders touched only by moonlight and his hands. She makes him burn with pleasure as no woman ever has, but Griff, still hurt by a betrayal he's never forgiven, insists he wants only a friend and a lover. Single and childless, Sharron has always been content with her life—until she thrills to the ecstacy Griff shows her, and now finds herself struggling with her need to be his wife and Harry's mother. Rest assured that a happily-ever-after awaits these two, as well as the young one, once they admit the love they can't deny. Victoria tells a compelling love story, one you won't be able to put down.

Who can resist **THE COURTING COWBOY**, LOVESWEPT #626 by Glenna McReynolds? Ty Garrett is a rough-edged rancher who wants a woman to share the seasons, to love under the Colorado skies. But he expects that finding a lady in his middle-of-nowhere town would be very rough—until a spirited visiting teacher fascinates his son and captivates him too! Victoria Willoughby has beautiful skin, a very kissable mouth, and a sensual innocence that beckons Ty to woo her with fierce, possessive passion. He awakens her to pleasures she's never imagined, teaches her how wonderful taking chances can be, and makes her feel alluring, wanton. But she's already let one man rule her life and she's vowed never to belong to anyone ever again. Still, she knows that finding Ty is a miracle; now if she'll only realize that he's the best man and the right man for her . . . Glenna's talent shines brightly in this terrific romance.

Bonnie Pega begins her deliciously sexy novel, **THEN COMES MARRIAGE**, LOVESWEPT #627, with the hero and heroine meeting in a very unlikely place. Single mother-to-be Libby Austin certainly thinks that seeing the hunk of her dreams in a childbirth class is truly rotten luck, but she breathes a sigh of relief when she discovers that Zac Webster is coaching his sister-in-law, not his wife! His potent masculinity can charm every stitch of clothing off a woman's body; too bad he makes it all too clear that a child doesn't fit into his life. Still, unable to resist the temptation of Libby's blue velvet eyes and delectable smile, Zac lays siege to her senses, and her response of torrential kisses and fevered caresses drive him even wilder with hunger. Libby has given him more than he's hoped for—and a tricky dilemma. Can a man who's sworn off marriage and vows he's awful with kids claim a wildfire bride and her baby? With this wonderful romance, her second LOVESWEPT, Bonnie proves that she's a name to watch for.

There's no sexier **MAN AROUND THE HOUSE** than the hero in Cindy Gerard's upcoming LOVESWEPT, #628. Matthew Spencer is a lean, muscled heartbreaker, and when he answers his new next-door neighbor's cries for help, he finds himself rescuing disaster-prone Katie

McDonald, who's an accident waiting to happen—and a sassy temptress who's sure to keep him up nights. Awakening his hunger with the speed of a summer storm, Katie senses his pain and longs to comfort him, but Matthew makes her feel too much, makes her want more than she can have. Though she lets herself dare to dream of being loved, Katie knows she's all wrong for a man who's walking a careful path to regain custody of his son. He needs nice and normal, not her kind of wild and reckless—no matter that they sizzle in each other's arms. But Matthew's not about to give up a woman who adores his child, listens to his favorite golden oldie rock station, and gives him kisses that knock his socks off and make the stars spin. The magic of Cindy's writing shines through in this enchanting tale of love.

Finishing the line-up in a big way is Marcia Evanick and **IN DADDY'S ARMS**, LOVESWEPT #629. Brave enough to fight back from wounds inflicted in the line of duty, Bain O'Neill is devastated when doctors tell him he'll never be a father. Having a family is the only dream that ever mattered to him, a fantasy he can't give up, not when he knows that somewhere there are two children who are partly his, the result of an anonymous sperm donation he made years ago. A little investigation helps him locate his daughters—and their mother, Erin Flynn, a fiery-haired angel who tastes as good as she looks. Widowed for two years, Erin takes his breath away and heals him with her loving touch. Bain hates keeping the truth from her, and though the children soon beg him to be their daddy, he doesn't dare confess his secret to Erin, not until he's silenced her doubts about his love and makes her believe he's with her to stay forever. All the stirring emotions and funny touches that you've come to expect from Marcia are in this fabulous story.

On sale this month from Bantam are three spectacular women's novels. Dianne Edouard and Sandra Ware have teamed up once again and written **SACRED LIES,** a spellbinding novel of sin, seduction, and betrayal. Romany Chase is the perfect spy: intelligent, beautiful, a woman who thrills to the hunt. But with her latest mission, Romany is out of her depth. Adrift in a world where redemption may arrive too late, she is torn between the enigmatic priest she has orders to seduce and the fierce agent she desires. Beneath the glittering Roman moon, a deadly conspiracy of greed, corruption, and shattering evil is closing in, and Romany must choose whom to believe—and whom to love.

With more than several million copies of her novels in print, Kay Hooper is indisputably one of the best loved and popular authors of romantic fiction—and now she has penned **THE WIZARD OF SEATTLE,** a fabulous, magical story of immortal love and mesmerizing fantasy. Serena Smyth travels cross-country to Seattle to find Richard Patrick Merlin, guided by an instinct born of her determination to become a master wizard like him. She knows he can be her teacher, but she never expects the fire he ignites in her body and soul. Their love forbidden by an ancient law, Serena and Merlin will take a desperate gamble and travel to the long-lost world of Atlantis—to change the history that threatens to keep them apart for eternity.

From bestselling author Susan Johnson comes **SILVER FLAME,** the steamy sequel about the Braddock-Black dynasty you read about in **BLAZE.** Pick up a copy and find out why *Romantic Times* gave the author its Best Sensual Historical Romance Award. Sizzling with electrifying sensuality, **SILVER FLAME** burns hot! When Empress

Jordan is forced to sell her most precious possession to the highest bidder in order to feed her brothers and sisters, Trey Braddock-Black knows he must have her, no matter what the cost. The half-Absarokee rogue has no intention of settling down with one woman, but once he's spent three weeks with the sweet enchantress, he knows he can never give her up. . . .

Also on sale this month, in the hardcover edition from Doubleday, is **THE PAINTED LADY,** the stunningly sensual debut novel by Lucia Grahame. All of Paris and London recognize Fleur not only as Frederick Brooks's wife, but also as the successful painter's most inspiring model. But few know the secrets behind his untimely death and the terrible betrayal that leaves Fleur with a heart of ice—and no choice but to accept Sir Anthony Camwell's stunning offer: a fortune to live on in return for five nights of unrestrained surrender to what he plans to teach her—the exquisite art of love.

Happy reading!

With warmest wishes,

Nita Taublib

Nita Taublib
Associate Publisher
LOVESWEPT and FANFARE

Don't miss these exciting
books by your favorite
Bantam authors
On Sale in May:

SACRED LIES
by Dianne Edouard
and Sandra Ware

THE WIZARD OF SEATTLE
by Kay Hooper

SILVER FLAME
by Susan Johnson

"SPECIAL SNEAK PREVIEW"
THE MAGNIFICENT ROGUE
by Iris Johansen
On Sale in August

SACRED LIES
by Dianne Edouard and Sandra Ware

On Sale in May

Romany Chase is the perfect spy: intelligent, beautiful, a woman who thrills to the hunt. But torn between the fierce Israeli agent she desires and the enigmatic priest she has orders to seduce, Romany is out of her depth—adrift in a world where redemption may arrive too late . . . .

As soon as Romany opened the door, she knew she wasn't alone. Someone waited for her. Somewhere in the apartment.

She had never carried a gun. There had never been a need. Even though Sully could have gotten her easy clearance, and had more than once urged her to take along some insurance. But her assignments never warranted it. Except that one time, in Geneva, and that situation had come totally out of left field.

She allowed her eyes to become adjusted to the gloom and, easing herself against the wall, moved to the edge of the living room. She searched the shadows. Strained to see something behind the thick lumps and bumps of furniture. Nothing. She crouched lower and inched closer to the door opening into her bedroom.

She peered around the corner. Whoever was in the apartment had switched on the ceiling fan and the small lamp that sat on a dressing table in the adjoining bath. The soft light cast the room in semidarkness, and she could make out the large solid shape of a man. He reclined easily upon her bed, a marshmallowy heap of pillows propped against his back. He hadn't bothered to draw back the covers, and he lay on top of the spread completely naked.

She should have run, gotten out of her apartment as quickly as possible. Except she recognized the hard muscles under the deeply tanned skin, the black curling hair, the famous smirk that passed for a smile. Recognized the man who was a cold-blooded killer—and her lover.

Romany moved through the doorway and smiled. "I'm not even going to ask how you got in here, David."

She heard his dark laugh. "Is that any way to greet an old friend?"

She walked farther into the room and stood by the side of the bed. She stared into the bright green eyes, still a surprise after all this time. But then everything about David ben Haar was a surprise. "Why don't you make yourself comfortable?"

"I am . . . almost." He reached for her hand and ran it slowly down his chest, stopping just short of the black hair at his groin.

She glanced down, focusing on her hand, pale and thin clasped inside his. She could hear her breath catch inside her throat. And as if that sound had been meant as some sort of signal, he pulled her down beside him.

She rested with her back against him, letting him work the muscles at her shoulders, brush his lips against her hair. She didn't turn when she finally decided to speak. "What are you doing here, David?"

"I came to see you." The words didn't sound like a complete lie.

She twisted herself round to look up at him. "That's terribly flattering, David, but it won't work."

She watched the smirk almost stretch into a real smile.

"Okay, I came to make sure that Sully is taking good care of my girl."

"I'm not your girl, David." She tried not to sound mean, or hurt, or anything. But she could feel the muscles of his stomach tighten against her back.

"You know Sully's a fucking asshole," he said finally. "What's he waiting on, those jerks to open up a concentration camp and gas a few thousand Jews?"

"David, Sully's not an asshole. . . . Hey, what in the hell do you mean?" She jerked around, waiting for an answer, watching his eyes turn cold.

"Gimme a break, Romany."

"Dammit, David, I don't have the slightest idea what you're talking about. Besides, what in the hell have concentration camps got to do with . . . ?" She stopped short, not willing to play her hand, even though David probably knew all the cards she was holding.

"Well, Romany, I can save you, and Sully, and all your little friends over at the CIA a whole helluva lotta trouble. Somebody—and I think you're deaf, dumb, and blind if you haven't pegged who that is—is stealing the Church blind, swiping paintings right off the museum walls, then slipping by some pretty goddamn good fakes."

She watched him stare at her from inside the darkness of her bed, waiting with that flirting smirk on his mouth for her to say something. But she didn't answer.

" . . . And the SOB at the other end of this operation"—he was finishing what he'd started—"whether your CIA geniuses want to admit it or not, is black-marketing the genuine articles, funneling the profits to a group of neo-Nazis who aren't going to settle for German reunification."

"Neo-Nazis?"

She could hear him grit his teeth. "Yeah, neo-Nazis. Getting East and West Germany together was just the first stage of their nasty little operation. They've got big plans, Romany. But they're the same old fuckers. Just a little slicker."

"David, I can't believe—"

"Shit, you people never want to believe—"

"Stop it, David."

He dropped his head and took in a deep staccatoed breath. She felt his hands move up her arms to her shoulders and force her body close to his. "Sorry, Romany." He sounded hoarse. Then suddenly she felt him laughing against her. "You know something"—he was drawing back—"you're on the wrong side, Romany. We wouldn't have these stupid fights if you'd come and work with me. With the Mossad."

"Yeah? Work with you, huh? And just what inducement can you offer, David ben Haar?" She pulled away from him and stood up.

Her feelings about David were a tangled mess—which, after she'd watched him board the plane for Tel Aviv thirteen months ago, she'd thought she could safely leave unwound. But here he was again, still looking at her with that quizzical twist to his lips that she couldn't help but read as a challenge.

She wanted his hands on her. That was the thought that kept repeating itself, blotting out everything else in her mind. Her own hands trembled as she pushed the hair away from her neck and began to undo the buttons at her back. Undressing for him slowly, the way he liked it.

She hadn't let herself know how much she'd missed this, until she was beneath the covers naked beside him, and his hands were really on her again, taking control, his mouth moving everywhere on her body. The pulse of the ceiling fan blended suddenly with the rush of blood in her ears, and David's heat was under her skin like fire.

She pressed herself closer against him, her need for him blocking out her doubts. She wanted his solidness, his back under her hands, the hardness of him along the length of her body. David ben Haar, the perfect sexual fantasy. But real. Flesh and blood with eyes green as the sea. She looked into his eyes as he pulled her beneath him. There was no lightness in them now, only the same intensity of passion as when he killed. He came into her hard, and she shut her eyes, matching her rhythm to his. To dream was all right, as long as you didn't let it go beyond the borders of your bed.

* * *

With one small edge of the curtain rolled back, David ben Haar could just see through the balcony railing where the red Alfa Romeo Spider was waiting to park in the street. Romany had been flying about the apartment when the car had first driven up, still cursing him for her half-damp hair, amusingly anxious to keep the priest from getting as far as her door.

"I could hide in the bedroom." He had said it from his comfortable position, lying still naked on her sofa. Laughing at her as she went past buttoning her dress, hobbling on one shoe back to the bedroom.

"I don't trust you, David ben Haar." She'd come back with her other shoe and was throwing a hairbrush into that satchel she called a purse.

"Romany?" He had concentrated on the intent face, the wild curls threatening to break loose from the scarf that bound them. "Morrow one of the bad guys?"

Picking up a sweater, she had looked over at him then, with something remarkably like guilt. "I don't know." She was going for the door. "That's what I'm supposed to find out."

Then she was gone, her heels rat-tatting down the stairs. High heels at Villa d'Este. Just like an American. They never took anything seriously, then covered it up with a cynicism they hadn't earned. Romany was the flip side of that, of course, all earnestness and innocence. She was smart and she had guts. But it wouldn't be enough to protect her. He got up.

As he watched now, the Spider was swinging into the parking space that had finally become available at the curb. The door opened and a man got out, turning to where Romany had just emerged from under the balcony overhang. The man didn't exactly match the car, he looked far too American. What he didn't look like was a priest.

He watched them greet each other. Very friendly. The compressor on the air conditioner picked that minute to kick in again, so he couldn't hope to hear what was said. The man opened the passenger door for her, then walked around to get in. They didn't pull out right away, and he was wondering why when he saw the canvas top go down. The engine roared up as they shot away from the curb. He could tell by the tilt of her head that Romany was laughing.

They had not spoken for some time now, standing among the tall cypress, looking out below to the valley. The dying sun had painted everything in a kind of saturated light, and he seemed almost surreal standing next to her, his fair aureole of hair and tall body in light-colored shirt and slacks glowing against the blackness of the trees.

They had played today, she and Julian Morrow. Like happy strangers who had met in Rome, with no history and no future. She had felt it immediately, the playfulness, implicit in the red car, in the way he wore the light, casual clothes. Like an emblem, like a costume at a party.

She had sat in the red car, letting the wind blow everything away from her mind, letting it rip David from her body. Forgetting the job. Forgetting that the man beside her was a priest and a suspect, and she a paid agent of the United States government.

They had played today. And she had liked this uncomplicated persona better than any he had so far let her see. Liked his ease and his sense of humor, and the pleasure he had seemed to find in their joyful sharing of this place. She had to stop playing now, but this was the Julian Morrow she must hold in her mind. Not the priest. Not the suspect in criminal forgery. But a Julian Morrow to whom she could want to make love.

He turned to her and smiled. For a moment the truth of her treachery rose to stick in her throat. But she forced it down. This was her job. She was committed.

She smiled back, moving closer, as if she might want a better view, or perhaps some little shelter from the wind. He must have thought the latter, because she felt his hands draping her sweater more firmly around her shoulders.

Time to take the advantage. And shifting backward, she pressed herself lightly against his chest, her eyes closed. She was barely breathing, feeling for any answering strain. But she could find no sense of any rejection in his posture.

She turned. He was looking down at her. His eyes, so close, were unreadable. She would never remember exactly what had happened next, but she knew when her arms went around him. And the small moment of her triumph when she felt him hard against her. Then she was pulling him down toward her, her fingers tangling in his hair, her mouth moving on his.

At the moment when she ceased thinking at all, he let her go, suddenly, with a gesture almost brutal that set her tumbling back. His hand reached for her wrist, didn't let her fall. But the grip was not kind or gentle.

His face was closed. Completely. Anger would have been better. She was glad when he turned away from her, walking back in the direction of the car. There would be no dinner tonight at the wonderful terraced restaurant he had talked about today. Of that she was perfectly sure. It was going to be a long drive back to Rome.

THE WIZARD OF SEATTLE
the unique new romantic fantasy from
Kay Hooper

On Sale in May

In the bestselling tradition of the time-travel romances of Diana Gabaldon and Constance O'Day-Flannery, Kay Hooper creates her own fabulous, magical story of timeless love and mesmerizing fantasy.

She looked like a ragged, storm-drenched urchin, but from the moment Serena Smyth appeared on his Seattle doorstep Richard Patrick Merlin recognized the spark behind her green eyes, the wild talent barely held in check. And he would help her learn to control her gift, despite a taboo so ancient that the reasons for its existence had been forgotten. But he never suspected that in his rebellion he would risk all he had and all he was to feel a love none of his kind had ever known.

Seattle, 1984

It was his home. She knew that, although where her certainty came from was a mystery to her. Like the inner tug that had drawn her across the country to find him, the knowledge seemed instinctive, beyond words or reason. She didn't even know his name. But she knew what he was. He was what she wanted to be, needed to be, what all her instincts insisted she had to be, and only he could teach her what she needed to learn.

Until this moment, she had never doubted that he would accept her as his pupil. At sixteen, she was passing through that stage of development experienced by humans, twice in their lifetimes, a stage marked by total self-absorption and the unshakable certainty that the entire universe revolves around oneself. It occurred in infancy and in adolescence, but rarely ever again, unless one were utterly unconscious of reality. Those traits had given her the confidence she had needed in order to cross the country alone with no more than a ragged backpack and a few dollars.

But they deserted her now, as she stood at the wrought iron gates and stared up at the secluded old Victorian house. The rain beat down on her, and lightning flashed in the stormy sky, illuminating the turrets and gables of the house; there were few lighted windows, and those were dim rather than welcoming.

It *looked* like the home of a wizard.

She almost ran, abruptly conscious of her aloneness. But then she squared her thin shoulders, shoved open the gate, and walked steadily to the front door. Ignoring the bell, she used the brass knocker to rap sharply. The knocker was fashioned in the shape of an owl, the creature that symbolized wisdom, a familiar of wizards throughout fiction.

She didn't know about fact.

Her hand was shaking, and she gave it a fierce frown as she rapped the knocker once more against the solid door. She barely had time to release the knocker before the door was pulled open.

Tall and physically powerful, his raven hair a little shaggy and his black eyes burning with an inner fire, he surveyed the dripping, ragged girl on his doorstep with lofty disdain for long moments during which all of her determination melted away to nothing. Then he caught her collar with one elegant hand, much as he might have grasped a stray cat, and yanked her into the well-lit entrance hall. He studied her with daunting sternness.

What he saw was an almost painfully thin girl who looked much younger than her sixteen years. Her threadbare clothing was soaked; her short, tangled hair was so wet that only a hint of its normal vibrant red color was apparent; and her small face—all angles and seemingly filled with huge eyes—was white and pinched. She was no more attractive than a stray mongrel pup.

"Well?"

The vast poise of sixteen years deserted the girl as he barked the one word in her ear. She gulped. "I—I want to be a wizard," she managed finally, defiantly.

"Why?"

She was soaked to the skin, tired, hungry, and possessed a temper that had more than once gotten her into trouble. Her green eyes snapping, she glared up into his handsome, expressionless face, and her voice lost all its timidity.

"I *will* be a wizard! If you won't teach me, I'll find someone who will. I can summon fire already—a little—and I can *feel* the power inside me. All I need is a teacher, and I'll be great one day—"

He lifted her clear off the floor and shook her briefly, effortlessly, inducing silence with no magic at all. "The first lesson an apprentice must learn," he told her calmly, "is to never—ever—shout at a Master."

Then he casually released her, conjured a bundle of clothing out of thin air, and handed it to her. Then he waved a hand negligently and sent her floating up the dark stairs toward a bathroom.

And so it began.

Seattle, Present

His fingers touched her breasts, stroking soft skin and teasing the hard pink nipples. The swollen weight filled his hands as he lifted and kneaded, and when she moaned and arched her back, he lowered his mouth to her. He stopped thinking.

He felt. He felt his own body, taut and pulsing with desire, the blood hot in his veins. He felt her body, soft and warm and willing. He felt her hand on him, stroking slowly, her touch hungry and assured. Her moans and sighs filled his ears, and the heat of her need rose until her flesh burned. The tension inside him coiled more tightly, making his body ache, until he couldn't stand to wait another moment. He sank his flesh into hers, feeling her legs close strongly about his hips. Expertly, lustfully, she met his thrusts, undulating beneath him, her female body the cradle all men returned to. The heat between them built until it was a fever raging out of control, until his body was gripped by the inescapable, inexorable drive for release and pounded frantically inside her. Then, at last, the heat and tension drained from him in a rush . . .

Serena sat bolt upright in bed, gasping. In shock, she stared across the darkened room for a moment, and then she hurriedly leaned over and turned on the lamp on the nightstand. Blinking in the light, she held her hands up and stared at them, reassuring herself that they were hers, still slender and pale and tipped with neat oval nails.

They were hers. She was here and unchanged. Awake. Aware. Herself again.

She could still feel the alien sensations, still see the powerful bronzed hands against paler, softer skin, and still feel sensations her body was incapable of experiencing simply because she was female, not male—

And then she realized.

"Dear God . . . Richard," she whispered.

She had been inside his mind, somehow, in his head just like before, and he had been with another woman. He had been having sex with another woman. Serena had felt what he felt, from the sensual enjoyment of soft female flesh under his touch to the ultimate draining pleasure of orgasm. *She had felt what he felt.*

She drew her knees up and hugged them, feeling tears burning her eyes and nausea churning in her stomach. Another woman. He had a woman somewhere, and she wasn't new because there had been a sense of familiarity in him, a certain knowledge. He knew this woman. Her skin was familiar, her taste, her desire. His body knew hers.

Even Master wizards, it seemed, had appetites just like other men.

Serena felt a wave of emotions so powerful she could endure them only in silent anguish. Her thoughts were tangled and fierce and raw. Not a monk, no, hardly a monk. In fact, it appeared he was quite a proficient lover, judging by the woman's response to him.

On her nightstand, the lamp's bulb burst with a violent sound, but she neither heard it nor noticed the return of darkness to the room.

So he was just a man after all, damn him, a man who got horny like other men and went to some woman who'd spread her legs for him. And often. His trips "out of town" were more frequent these last years. Oh, horny indeed . . .

Unnoticed by Serena, her television set flickered to life, madly scanned though all the channels, and then died with a sound as apologetic as a muffled cough.

Damn him. What'd he do, keep a mistress? Some pretty, pampered blonde—she had been blond, naturally—with empty hot eyes who wore slinky nightgowns and crotchless panties, and moaned like a bitch in heat? Was there only one? Or had he bedded a succession of women over the years, keeping his reputation here in Seattle all nice and tidy while he satisfied his appetites elsewhere?

Serena heard a little sound, and was dimly shocked to realize it came from her throat. It sounded like that of an animal in pain, some tortured creature hunkered down in the dark as it waited helplessly to find out if it would live or die. She didn't realize that she was rocking gently. She didn't see her alarm clock flash a series of red numbers before going dark, or notice that her stereo system was spitting out tape from a cassette.

Only when the overhead light suddenly exploded was Serena jarred from her misery. With a tremendous effort, she struggled to control herself.

"Concentrate," she whispered. "Concentrate. Find the switch." And, for the first time, perhaps spurred on by her urgent need to control what she felt, she did find it. Her wayward energies stopped swirling all around her and were instantly drawn into some part of her she'd never recognized before, where they were completely and safely contained, held there in waiting without constant effort from her.

Moving stiffly, feeling exhausted, Serena got out of bed and moved cautiously across the room to her closet, trying to avoid the shards of glass sprinkled over the rugs and the polished wood floor. There were extra lightbulbs on the closet shelf, and she took one to replace the one from her nightstand lamp. It was difficult to unscrew the burst bulb, but she managed; she didn't trust herself to flick all the shattered pieces out of existence with her powers, not when she'd come so close to losing control entirely.

When the lamp was burning again, she got a broom and dustpan and cleaned up all the bits of glass. A slow survey of the room revealed what else she had destroyed, and she shivered a little at the evidence of just how dangerous unfocused power could be.

Ironically, she couldn't repair what she had wrecked, not by using the powers that had destroyed. Because she didn't understand the technology of television or radio or even clocks, it simply wasn't possible for her to focus her powers to fix what was broken. It would be like the blind trying to put together by touch alone something they couldn't even recognize enough to define.

To create or control anything, it was first necessary to understand its very elements, its basic structure, and how it functioned. How many times had Merlin told her that? Twenty times? A hundred?

Serena sat down on her bed, still feeling drained. But not numb; that mercy wasn't granted to her. The switch she had found to contain her energies could do nothing to erase the memory of Richard with another woman.

It hurt. She couldn't believe how much it hurt. All these years she had convinced herself that she was the only woman in his life who mattered, and now she knew that wasn't true. He didn't belong only to her. He didn't belong to her at all. He really didn't see her as a woman—or, if he did, she obviously held absolutely no attraction for him.

The pain was worse, knowing that.

Dawn had lightened the windows by the time Serena tried to go back to sleep. But she couldn't. She lay beneath the covers staring up at the ceiling, feeling older than she had ever felt before. There was no limbo now, no sense of being suspended between woman and child; Serena knew she could never again be a child, not even to protect herself.

The question was—how was that going to alter her relationship with Merlin? Could she pretend there was nothing different? No. Could she even bear to look at him without crying out her pain and rage? Probably not. How would he react when she made her feelings plain, with disgust or pity? That was certainly possible. Would her raw emotion drive him even farther away from her? Or was he, even now, planning to banish her from his life completely?

Because he knew. He knew what she had discovered in the dark watches of the night.

Just before her own shock had wrenched her free of his mind, Serena had felt for a split-second *his* shock as he sensed and recognized her presence intruding on that intensely private act.

He knew. He knew she had been there.

It was another part of her pain, the discomfiting guilt and

shame of having been, however unintentionally, a voyeur. She had a memory now that she would never forget, but it was his, not hers. She'd stolen it from ˙im . . . . And of all the things they both had to face when he ˙me home, that one was likely to be the most difficult of all.

The only certainty Serena could find in any of it was the knowledge that nothing would ever be the same again.

SILVER FLAME
by Susan Johnson

On Sale in May

She was driven by love to break every rule.... Empress
Jordan had fled to the Montana wilderness to escape a cruel
injustice, only to find herself forced to desperate means to
feed her brothers and sisters. Once she agreed to sell her most
precious possession to the highest bidder, she feared she'd made
a terrible mistake—even as she found herself hoping it was the
tall, dark, chiseled stranger who had taken her dare and claimed
her ....

Empress stood before him, unabashed in her nudity, and
raising her emerald eyes the required height to meet his so
far above, she said "What *will* you do with me, Mr. Braddock-
Black?"

"Trey," he ordered, unconscious of his lightly command-
ing tone.

"What *will* you do with me, Trey?" she repeated correcting
herself as ordered. But there was more than a hint of impudence in her tone and in her tilted mouth and arched brow.

Responding to the impudence with some of his own, he
replied with a small smile, "Whatever you prefer, Empress,
darling." He towered over her, clothed and booted, as dark
as Lucifer, and she was intensely aware of his power and size,
as if his presence seemed to invade her. "You set the pace,
sweetheart," he said encouragingly, reaching out to slide the

pad of one finger slowly across her shoulder. "But take your time," he went on, recognizing his own excitement, running his warm palm up her neck and cupping the back of her head lightly. Trey's voice had dropped half an octave. "We've three weeks. . . ." And for the first time in his life he looked forward to three undiluted weeks of one woman's company. It was like scenting one's mate, primordial and reflexive, and while his intellect ignored the peremptory, inexplicable compulsion, his body and blood and dragooned sensory receptors willingly complied to the urgency.

Bending his head low, his lips touched hers lightly, brushing twice across them like silken warmth before he gently slid over her mouth with his tongue and sent a shocking trail of fire curling deep down inside her.

She drew back in an unconscious response, but he'd felt the heated flame, too, and from the startled look in his eyes she knew the spark had touched them both. Trey's breathing quickened, his hand tightened abruptly on the back of her head, pulling her closer with insistence, with authority, while his other hand slid down her back until it rested warmly at the base of her spine. And when his mouth covered hers a second time, intense suddenly, more demanding, she could feel him rising hard against her. She may have been an innocent in the ways of a man and a woman, but Empress knew how animals mated in nature, and for the first time she sensed a soft warmth stirring within herself.

It was at once strange and blissful, and for a brief detached moment she felt very grown, as if a riddle of the universe were suddenly revealed. One doesn't have to love a man to feel the fire, she thought. It was at odds with all her mother had told her. Inexplicably she experienced an overwhelming sense of discovery, as if she alone knew a fundamental principle of humanity. But then her transient musing was abruptly arrested, for under the light pressure of Trey's lips she found hers opening, and the velvety, heated caress of Trey's tongue slowly entered her mouth, exploring languidly, licking her sweetness, and the heady, brandy taste of him was like a fresh treasure to be savored. She tentatively responded like a lambkin to new, unsteady legs, and when her tongue brushed his and did her own unhurried tasting, she heard him groan low in his throat. Swaying gently against her, his hard length pressed more adamantly into her yielding softness. Fire raced downward to a tingling place deep inside her as Trey's strong, insistent arousal throbbed against the soft curve of her stomach. He held her captive with his large hand low on her back as they kissed, and she felt a leaping flame speed along untried nerve endings, creating delicious new sensations. There was strange pleasure in the feel of his soft wool shirt; a melting warmth seeped through her senses, and she swayed closer into the strong male body, as if she knew instinctively that he would rarefy the enchantment. A moment later, as her mouth opened pliantly beneath his, her hands came up of their own accord and, rich with promise, rested lightly on his shoulders.

Her artless naîveté was setting his blood dangerously afire. He gave her high marks for subtlety. First the tentative withdrawal, and now the ingenuous response, was more erotic than any flagrant vice of the most skilled lover. And yet it surely must be some kind of drama, effective like the scene downstairs, where she withheld more than she offered in the concealing men's clothes and made every man in the room want to undress her.

Whether artifice, pretext, sham, or entreating supplication, the soft, imploring body melting into his, the small appealing hands warm on his shoulders, made delay suddenly inconvenient. "I think, sweet Empress," he said, his breath warm on her mouth, "*next* time you can set the pace. . . ."

Bending quickly, he lifted her into his arms and carried her to the bed. Laying her down on the rose velvet coverlet, he stood briefly and looked at her. Wanton as a Circe nymph, she looked back at him, her glance direct into his heated gaze, and she saw the smoldering, iridescent desire in his eyes. She was golden pearl juxtaposed to blush velvet, and when she slowly lifted her arms to him, he, no longer in control of himself, not detached or casual or playful as he usually was making love, took a deep breath, swiftly moved the half step to the bed, and lowered his body over hers, reaching for the buttons on his trousers with trembling fingers. His boots crushed the fine velvet but he didn't notice; she whimpered slightly when his heavy gold belt buckle pressed into her silken skin, but he kissed her in apology, intent on burying himself in the devastating Miss Jordan's lushly carnal body. His wool-clad legs pushed her pale thighs apart, and all he could think of was the feel of her closing around him. He surged forward, and she cried out softly. Maddened with desire, he thrust forward again. This time he *heard* her cry. "Oh, Christ," he breathed, urgent need suffocating in his lungs, "you can't be a virgin." He never bothered with virgins. It had been years since he'd slept with one. Lord, he was hard.

"It doesn't matter," she replied quickly, tense beneath him.

"It doesn't matter," he repeated softly, blood drumming in his temples and in his fingertips and in the soles of his feet inside the custom-made boots, and most of all in his rigid erection, insistent like a battering ram a hair's breadth from where he wanted to be so badly, he could taste the blood in his mouth. It doesn't matter, his conscience repeated. She said it doesn't matter, so it doesn't matter, and he drove in again.

Her muffled cry exploded across his lips as his mouth lowered to kiss her.

"Oh, hell." He exhaled deeply, drawing back, and, poised on his elbows, looked down at her uncertainly, his long dark hair framing his face like black silk.

"I won't cry out again," she whispered, her voice more certain than the poignant depths of her shadowy eyes. "Please . . . I must have the money."

It was all too odd and too sudden and too out of character for him. Damn . . . plundering a virgin, making her cry in fear and pain. *Steady, you'll live if you don't have her*, he told himself, but quivering need played devil's advocate to that platitude. She was urging him on. His body was even more fiercely demanding he take her. "Hell and damnation," he muttered disgruntledly. The problem was terrible, demanding immediate answers, and he wasn't thinking too clearly, only feeling a delirious excitement quite detached from moral judgment. And adamant. "Bloody hell," he breathed, and in that moment, rational thought gained a fingertip control on the ragged edges of his lust. "Keep the money. I don't want to—" He said it quickly, before he'd change his mind, then paused and smiled. "Obviously that's not entirely true, but I don't ruin virgins," he said levelly.

Empress had not survived the death of her parents and the months following, struggling to stay alive in the wilderness, without discovering in herself immense strength. She summoned it now, shakily but determinedly. "It's not a moral dilemma. It's a business matter and my responsibility. I insist."

He laughed, his smile close and deliciously warm. "Here I'm refusing a woman insisting I take her virginity. I must be crazy."

"The world's crazy sometimes, I think," she replied softly, aware of the complex reasons prompting her conduct.

"Tonight, at least," he murmured, "it's more off track than usual." But even for a wild young man notorious as a womanizer, the offered innocence was too strangely bizarre. And maybe too businesslike for a man who found pleasure and delight in the act. It was not flattering to be a surrogate for a business matter. "Look," he said with an obvious effort, "thanks but no thanks. I'm not interested. But keep the money. I admire your courage." And rolling off her, he lay on his back and shouted, "*Flo!*"

"No!" Empress cried, and was on top of him before he drew his next breath, terrified he'd change his mind about the money, terrified he'd change his mind in the morning when his head was clear and he woke up in Flo's arms. Fifty thousand dollars was a huge sum of money to give away on a whim, or to lose to some misplaced moral scruple. She must convince him to stay with her, then at least she could earn the money. Or at least try.

Lying like silken enchantment on his lean, muscled body, she covered his face with kisses. Breathless, rushing kisses, a young girls's simple closemouthed kisses. Then, in a flush of boldness, driven by necessity, a tentative dancing lick of her small tongue slid down his straight nose, to his waiting mouth. When her tongue lightly caressed the arched curve of his upper lip, his hands came up and closed on her naked shoulders, and he drew the teasing tip into his mouth. He sucked on it gently, slowly, as if he envisioned a lifetime without interruptions, until the small, sun-kissed shoulders beneath his hands trembled in tiny quivers.

Strange, fluttering wing beats sped through her heating blood, and a curious languor caused Empress to twine her arms around Trey's strong neck. But her heart was beating hard like the Indian drums whose sound carried far up to their hidden valley in summer, for fear outweighed languor still. He mustn't go to Flo. Slipping her fingers through the black luster of his long hair, ruffled in loose waves on his neck, she brushed her mouth along his cheek. "Please," she whispered near his ear, visions of her hope to save her family dashed by his reluctance, "stay with me." It was a simple plea, simply put. It was perhaps her last chance. Her lips traced the perfect curve of his ears, and his hands tightened their grip in response. "Say it's all right. Say I can stay. . . ." She was murmuring rapidly in a flurry of words.

How should he answer the half-shy, quicksilver words? Why was she insisting? Why did the flattery of a woman wanting him matter?

Then she shifted a little so her leg slid between his, a sensual, instinctive movement, and the smooth velvet of his masculinity rose against her thigh. It was warm, it was hot, and like a child might explore a new sensation, she moved her leg lazily up its length.

Trey's mouth went dry, and he couldn't convince himself that refusal was important any longer. He groaned, thinking, there are some things in life without answers. His hand was trembling when he drew her mouth back to his.

A moment later, when Flo knocked and called out his name, Empress shouted, "Go away!" And when Flo repeated his name, Trey's voice carried clearly through the closed door. "I'll be down later."

He was rigid but tense and undecided, and Empress counted on the little she knew about masculine desire to accomplish what her logical explanation hadn't. Being French, she was well aware that *amour* could be heated and fraught with urgent emotion, but she was unsure exactly about the degree of urgency relative to desire.

But she knew what had happened moments before when she'd tasted his mouth and recalled how he'd responded to her yielding softness, so she practiced her limited expertise with a determined persistence. She must be sure she had the money. And if it would assure her family their future, her virginity was paltry stuff in the bargain.

"Now let's begin again," she whispered.

THE MAGNIFICENT ROGUE
by Iris Johansen

On Sale in August

From the glittering court of Queen Elizabeth to the barren island of Craighdu, THE MAGNIFICENT ROGUE is the spellbinding story of courageous love and unspeakable evil. The daring chieftain of a Scottish clan, Robert MacDarren knows no fear, and only the threat to a kinsman's life makes him bow to Queen Elizabeth's order that he wed Kathryn Ann Kentrye. He's aware of the dangerous secret in Kate's past, a secret that could destroy a great empire, but he doesn't expect the stirring of desire when he first lays eyes on the fragile beauty. Grateful to escape the tyranny of her guardian, Kate accepts the mesmerizing stranger as her husband. But even as they discover a passion greater than either has known, enemies are weaving their poisonous web around them, and soon Robert and Kate must risk their very lives to defy the ultimate treachery.

In the following scene, Robert and his cousin Gavin Gordon have come to Kate's home to claim her—and she flees.

She was being followed!

Sebastian?

Kate paused a moment on the trail and caught a glimpse of dark hair and the shimmer of the gold necklace about her pursuer's neck. Not Sebastian. Robert MacDarren.

The wild surge of disappointment she felt at the realization was completely unreasonable. He must have come at Sebastian's bidding, which meant her guardian had persuaded him to his way of thinking. Well, what had she expected? He was a stranger and Sebastian was a respected man of the cloth. There was no reason why he would be different from any of the others. How clever of Sebastian to send someone younger and stronger than himself to search her out, she thought bitterly.

She turned and began to run, her shoes sinking into the mud with every step. She glanced over her shoulder.

He was closer. He was not running, but his long legs covered the ground steadily, effortlessly, as his gaze studied the trail in front of him. He had evidently not seen her yet and was only following her tracks.

She was growing weaker. Her head felt peculiarly light and her breath was coming in painful gasps. She couldn't keep running.

And she couldn't surrender.

Which left only one solution to her dilemma. She sprinted several yards ahead and then darted into the underbrush at the side of the trail.

Hurry. She had to hurry. Her gaze frantically searched the underbrush. Ah, there was one.

She pounced on a heavy branch and then backtracked several yards and held it, waiting.

She must aim for the head. She had the strength for only one blow and it must drop him.

Her breath sounded heavily and terribly loud. She had to breathe more evenly or he would hear her.

He was almost upon her.

Her hands tightened on the branch.

He went past her, his expression intent as he studied the tracks.

She drew a deep breath, stepped out on the trail behind him, and swung the branch with all her strength.

He grunted in pain and then slowly crumpled to the ground.

She dropped the branch and ran past his body and darted down the trail again.

Something struck the back of her knees. She was falling!

She hit the ground so hard, the breath left her body. Blackness swirled around her.

When the darkness cleared, she realized she was on her back, her arms pinned on each side of her head. Robert MacDarren was astride her body.

She started to struggle.

"Lie still, dammit." His hands tightened cruelly on her arms. "I'm not—Ouch!"

She had turned her head and sunk her teeth into his wrist. She could taste the coppery flavor of blood in her mouth, but his grip didn't ease.

"Let me go!" How stupidly futile the words were when she knew he had no intention of releasing her.

She tried to butt her head against his chest, but she couldn't reach him.

"Really, Robert, can't you wait until the words are said for you to climb on top of her?" Gavin Gordon said from behind MacDarren.

"It's about time you got here," MacDarren said in a growl. "She's trying to kill me."

'Aye, for someone who couldn't lift her head, she's doing quite well. I saw her strike the blow." Gavin grinned. "But I was too far away to come to your rescue. Did she do any damage?"

"I'm going to have one hell of a headache."

Kate tried to knee him in the groin, but he quickly moved upward on her body.

"Your hand's bleeding," Gavin observed.

"She's taken a piece out of me. I can see why Landfield kept the ropes on her."

The ropes. Despair tore through her as she realized how completely Sebastian had won him to his way of thinking. The man would bind her and take her back to Sebastian. She couldn't fight against both MacDarren and Gordon and would use the last of her precious strength trying to do so. She would have to wait for a better opportunity to present itself. She stopped fighting and lay there staring defiantly at him.

"Very sensible," MacDarren said grimly. "I'm not in a very good temper at the moment. I don't think you want to make it worse."

"Get off me."

"And have you run away again?" MacDarren shook his head. "You've caused me enough trouble for one day. Give me your belt, Gavin."

Gavin took off his wide leather belt and handed it to MacDarren, who buckled the belt about her wrists and drew it tight.

"I'm not going back to the cottage," she said with the fierceness born of desperation. "I *can't* go back there."

He got off her and rose to his feet. "You'll go where I tell you to go, even if I have to drag—" He stopped in self-disgust as he realized what he had said. "Christ, I sound like that bastard." The anger suddenly left him as he looked at her lying there before him. "You're afraid of him?"

Fear was always with her when she thought of Sebastian, but she would not admit it. She sat up and repeated, "I can't go back."

He studied her for a moment. "All right, we won't go back. You'll never have to see him again."

She stared at him in disbelief.

He turned to Gavin. "We'll stay the night at that inn we passed at the edge of the village. Go back to the cottage and get her belongings and then saddle the horses. We'll meet you at the stable."

Gavin nodded and the next moment disappeared into the underbrush.

MacDarren glanced down at Kate. "I trust you don't object to that arrangement?"

She couldn't comprehend his words. "You're taking me away?"

"If you'd waited, instead of jumping out the window, I would have told you that two hours ago. That's why I came."

Then she thought she understood. "You're taking me to the lady?"

He shook his head. "It appears Her Majesty thinks it's time you wed."

Shock upon shock. "Wed?"

He said impatiently, "You say that as if you don't know what it means. You must have had instructions on the duties of wifehood."

"I know what it means." Slavery and suffocation and cruelty. From what she could judge from Sebastian and Martha's marriage, a wife's lot was little better than her own. True, he did not beat Martha, but the screams she heard from their bedroom while they mated had filled her with sick horror. But she had thought she would never have to worry about that kind of mistreatment. "I can never marry."

"Is that what the good vicar told you?" His lips tightened. "Well, it appears the queen disagrees."

Then it might come to pass. Even Sebastian obeyed the queen. The faintest hope began to spring within her. Even though marriage was only another form of slavery, perhaps the queen had chosen an easier master than Sebastian for her. "Who am I to marry?"

He smiled sardonically. "I have that honor."

Another shock and not a pleasant one. Easy was not a term anyone would use to describe this man. She blurted, "And you're not afraid?"

"Afraid of you? Not if I have someone to guard my back."

That wasn't what she meant, but of course he wouldn't be afraid. She doubted if he feared anything or anyone, and, besides, she wasn't what Sebastian said she was. He had said the words so often, she sometimes found herself believing him, and she was so tired now, she wasn't thinking clearly. The strength was seeping out of her with every passing second. "No, you shouldn't be afraid." She swayed. "Not Lilith . . ."

"More like a muddy gopher," he muttered as he reached out and steadied her. "We have to get to the stable. Can you walk, or shall I carry you?"

"I can walk." She dismissed the outlandish thought of marriage from her mind. She would ponder the implications of this change in her life later. There were more important matters to consider now. "But we have to get Caird."

"Caird? Who the devil is Caird?"

"My horse." She turned and started through the underbrush. "Before we go I have to fetch him. He's not far. . . ."

She could hear the brush shift and whisper as he followed her. "Your horse is in the forest?"

"I was hiding him from Sebastian. He was going to kill him. He wanted me to tell him where he was."

"And that was why he was dragging you?"

She ignored the question. "Sebastian said the forest beasts would devour him. He frightened me." She was staggering with exhaustion, but she couldn't give up now. "It's been such a while since I left him." She rounded a corner of a trail and breathed a sigh of relief as she caught sight of Caird calmly munching grass under the shelter of an oak tree. "No, he's fine."

"You think so?" MacDarren's skeptical gaze raked the piebald stallion from its swayback to its knobby knees. "I see nothing fine about him. How old is he?"

"Almost twenty." She reached the horse and tenderly began to stroke his muzzle. "But he's strong and very good-tempered."

"He won't do," MacDarren said flatly. "We'll have to get rid of him. He'd never get through the Highlands. We'll leave him with the innkeeper and I'll buy you another horse."

"I *won't* get rid of him," she said fiercely. "I can't just leave him. How would I know if they'd take good care of him? He goes with us."

"And I say he stays."

The words were spoken with such absolute resolution that they sent a jolt of terror through her. They reminded her of Sebastian's edicts, from which there was no appeal. She moistened her lips. "Then I'll have to stay too."

MacDarren's gaze narrowed on her face. "And what if Landfield catches you again?"

She shrugged and leaned her cheek wearily against Caird's muzzle. "He belongs to me," she said simply.

She could feel his gaze on her back and sensed his exasperation. "Oh, for God's sake!" He picked up her saddle from the ground by the tree and threw it on Caird's back. He began to buckle the cinches. "All right, we'll take him."

Joy soared through her. "Truly?"

"I said it, didn't I?" He picked her up and tossed her into the saddle. "We'll use him as a pack horse and I'll get you another mount to ride. Satisfied?"

Satisfied! She smiled brilliantly. "Oh yes. You won't regret it. But you needn't spend your money on another horse. Caird is really very strong. I'm sure he'll be able to—"

"I'm already regretting it." His tone was distinctly edgy as he began to lead the horse through the forest. "Even carrying a light load, I doubt if he'll get through the Highlands."

It was the second time he had mentioned these forbidding Highlands, but she didn't care where they were going as long as they were taking Caird. "But you'll do it? You won't change your mind?"

For an instant his expression softened as he saw the eagerness in her face. "I won't change my mind."

Gavin was already mounted and waiting when they arrived at the stable a short time later. A grin lit his face as he glanced from Kate to the horse and then back again. "Hers?"

Robert nodded. "And the cause of all this turmoil."

"A fitting pair," Gavin murmured. "She has a chance of cleaning up decently, but the horse . . ." He shook his head. "No hope for it, Robert."

"My thought exactly. But we're keeping him anyway."

Gavin's brows lifted. "Oh, are we? Interesting . . ."

Robert swung into the saddle. "Any trouble with the vicar and his wife?"

Kate's hands tensed on the reins.

"Mistress Landfield appeared to be overjoyed to give me the girl's belongings." He nodded at a small bundle tied to the saddle. "And the vicar just glowered at me."

"Perhaps he's given up."

"He won't give up," Kate whispered. "He never gives up."

"Then perhaps we'd better go before we encounter him again," Robert said as he kicked his horse into a trot. "Keep an eye on her, Gavin. She's almost reeling in that saddle."

Sebastian was waiting for them a short distance from the cottage. He stood blocking the middle of the path.

"Get out of the way," Robert said coldly. "I'm not in the mood for this."

"It's your last chance," Sebastian said. "Give her back to me before it's too late."

"Stand aside, Landfield."

"Kathryn." Sebastian turned to her and his voice was pleading. "Do not go. You know you can never wed. You know what will happen."

Robert rode forward and his horse's shoulder forced Sebastian to the side of the trail. He motioned Gavin and Kate to ride ahead. "It's over. She's no longer your responsibility." His voice lowered to soft deadliness. "And if you ever approach her again, I'll make sure I never see you repeat the mistake."

"You'll see me." Landfield's eyes shimmered with tears as his gaze clung to Kate. "I wanted to spare you, Kathryn. I wanted to save you, but God has willed otherwise. You know what has to be done now."

He turned and walked heavily back toward the cottage.

"What did he mean?" Gavin asked as his curious gaze followed Landfield.

She didn't answer as she watched Sebastian stalk away. She realized she was shivering with a sense of impending doom. How foolish. This was what he wanted her to feel, his way of chaining her to him.

"Well?" Robert asked.

"Nothing. He just wanted to make me afraid." She moistened her lips. "He likes me to be afraid of him."

She could see he didn't believe her and thought he would pursue it. Instead he said quietly, "You don't have to fear him any longer. He no longer holds any power over you." He held her gaze with a mesmerizing power. "I'm the only one who does now."

OFFICIAL RULES TO WINNERS CLASSIC SWEEPSTAKES

No Purchase necessary. To enter the sweepstakes follow instructions found elsewhere in this offer. You can also enter the sweepstakes by hand printing your name, address, city, state and zip code on a 3" x 5" piece of paper and mailing it to: Winners Classic Sweepstakes, P.O. Box 785, Gibbstown, NJ 08027. Mail each entry separately. Sweepstakes begins 12/1/91. Entries must be received by 6/1/93. Some presentations of this sweepstakes may feature a deadline for the Early Bird prize. If the offer you receive does, then to be eligible for the Early Bird prize your entry must be received according to the Early Bird date specified. Not responsible for lost, late, damaged, misdirected, illegible or postage due mail. Mechanically reproduced entries are not eligible. All entries become property of the sponsor and will not be returned.

Prize Selection/Validations: Winners will be selected in random drawings on or about 7/30/93, by VENTURA ASSOCIATES, INC., an independent judging organization whose decisions are final. Odds of winning are determined by total number of entries received. Circulation of this sweepstakes is estimated not to exceed 200 million. Entrants need not be present to win. All prizes are guaranteed to be awarded and delivered to winners. Winners will be notified by mail and may be required to complete an affidavit of eligibility and release of liability which must be returned within 14 days of date of notification or alternate winners will be selected. Any guest of a trip winner will also be required to execute a release of liability. Any prize notification letter or any prize returned to a participating sponsor, Bantam Doubleday Dell Publishing Group, Inc., its participating divisions or subsidiaries, or VENTURA ASSOCIATES, INC. as undeliverable will be awarded to an alternate winner. Prizes are not transferable. No multiple prize winners except as may be necessary due to unavailability, in which case a prize of equal or greater value will be awarded. Prizes will be awarded approximately 90 days after the drawing. All taxes, automobile license and registration fees, if applicable, are the sole responsibility of the winners. Entry constitutes permission (except where prohibited) to use winners' names and likenesses for publicity purposes without further or other compensation.

Participation: This sweepstakes is open to residents of the United States and Canada, except for the province of Quebec. This sweepstakes is sponsored by Bantam Doubleday Dell Publishing Group, Inc. (BDD), 666 Fifth Avenue, New York, NY 10103. Versions of this sweepstakes with different graphics will be offered in conjunction with various solicitations or promotions by different subsidiaries and divisions of BDD. Employees and their families of BDD, its division, subsidiaries, advertising agencies, and VENTURA ASSOCIATES, INC., are not eligible.

Canadian residents, in order to win, must first correctly answer a time limited arithmetical skill testing question. Void in Quebec and wherever prohibited or restricted by law. Subject to all federal, state, local and provincial laws and regulations.

Prizes: The following values for prizes are determined by the manufacturers' suggested retail prices or by what these items are currently known to be selling for at the time this offer was published. Approximate retail values include handling and delivery of prizes. Estimated maximum retail value of prizes: 1 Grand Prize ($27,500 if merchandise or $25,000 Cash); 1 First Prize ($3,000); 5 Second Prizes ($400 each); 35 Third Prizes ($100 each); 1,000 Fourth Prizes ($9.00 each) ; 1 Early Bird Prize ($5,000); Total approximate maximum retail value is $50,000. Winners will have the option of selecting any prize offered at level won. Automobile winner must have a valid driver's license at the time the car is awarded. Trips are subject to space and departure availability. Certain black-out dates may apply. Travel must be completed within one year from the time the prize is awarded. Minors must be accompanied by an adult. Prizes won by minors will be awarded in the name of parent or legal guardian.

For a list of Major Prize Winners (available after 7/30/93): send a self-addressed, stamped envelope entirely separate from your entry to: Winners Classic Sweepstakes Winners, P.O. Box 825, Gibbstown, NJ 08027. Requests must be received by 6/1/93. DO NOT SEND ANY OTHER CORRESPONDENCE TO THIS P.O. BOX.

The Very Best In Contemporary Women's Fiction

Sandra Brown

_____	29085-1	22 INDIGO PLACE .... $4.50/5.50 in Canada
_____	56045-X	TEMPERATURES RISING $5.99/6.99
_____	28990-X	TEXAS! CHASE $5.99/6.99
_____	28951-9	TEXAS! LUCKY $5.99/6.99
_____	29500-4	TEXAS! SAGE $5.99/6.99
_____	29783-X	A WHOLE NEW LIGHT $5.99/6.99

Tami Hoag

_____	29534-9	LUCKY'S LADY $4.99/ 5.99
_____	29053-3	MAGIC $4.99/ 5.99
_____	29272-2	STILL WATERS $4.99/ 5.99
_____	56050-6	SARAH'S SIN $4.50/ 5.50

Nora Roberts

_____	27283-7	BRAZEN VIRTUE $4.99/5.99
_____	29597-7	CARNAL INNOCENCE $5.50/6.50
_____	29490-3	DIVINE EVIL $5.99/6.99
_____	29078-9	GENUINE LIES $4.99/5.99
_____	26461-3	HOT ICE $4.99/5.99
_____	28578-5	PUBLIC SECRETS $4.95/5.95
_____	26574-1	SACRED SINS $5.50/6.50
_____	27859-2	SWEET REVENGE $5.50/6.50

Pamela Simpson

_____	29424-5	FORTUNE'S CHILD $5.99/6.99

Deborah Smith

_____	29690-6	BLUE WILLOW $5.50/ 6.50
_____	29092-4	FOLLOW THE SUN $4.99/ 5.99
_____	29107-6	MIRACLE $4.50/ 5.50

Ask for these titles at your bookstore or use this page to order.

Please send me the books I have checked above. I am enclosing $ _____ (add $2.50 to
cover postage and handling). Send check or money order, no cash or C. O. D.'s please.

Mr./ Ms. _____

Address _____

City/ State/ Zip _____

Send order to: Bantam Books, Dept. FN24, 2451 S. Wolf Road, Des Plaines, IL 60018
Please allow four to six weeks for delivery.

Prices and availability subject to change without notice.

FN 24 - 3/93